Anonymous

Souvenir of modern minstrelsy

A collection of original and select poetry by living writers. 2d series

Anonymous

Souvenir of modern minstrelsy
A collection of original and select poetry by living writers. 2d series

ISBN/EAN: 9783337278588

Printed in Europe, USA, Canada, Australia, Japan

Cover: Foto ©Andreas Hilbeck / pixelio.de

More available books at **www.hansebooks.com**

SOUVENIR

OF

𝔐𝔬𝔡𝔢𝔯𝔫 𝔐𝔦𝔫𝔰𝔱𝔯𝔢𝔩𝔰𝔶.

A COLLECTION OF ORIGINAL AND SELECT POETRY
BY LIVING WRITERS.

SECOND SERIES.

LONDON:
SAMPSON LOW, SON, & CO., 47, LUDGATE HILL.
1861.

PREFACE.

ONCE more we present our readers with our annual bouquet of the flowers of poetry of the year, blended with which will be found a few imperishable blossoms gathered, by permission, from garlands woven long ago by Poets who are still living among us. To those who have contributed "*fresh flowers* from the garden of the heart," as well as to those who have so courteously and obligingly responded to our requests for a few blossoms from their own collections, the Editor would express his grateful acknowledgements; at the same time observing that, deploring the wholesale piracy of many compilers, he has carefully avoided quoting from the works of any writer without permission.

Should the names of any living Poets be found wanting, whose contributions would have lent additional graces to the volume, such omissions must not in all cases be attributed to the Editor's neglect, permission having sometimes been withheld, or often restricted to a single extract. Thanks, however, are

unfeignedly offered to those Poets and Publishers who
have so materially assisted us, and to the Public and
the Press for the generous reception given to our first
volume.   It is not our intention to remain satisfied
with present success, to relax in our efforts to promote
poetical literature, or cease to aid and encourage those
Poets who, without such a publication, would be
unable to introduce their writings to the Public.—
We invite, therefore, the assistance of authors, known
and unknown ; and as an expression of our determina-
tion to improve our publication, we have commenced,
as a new feature. a series of illustrations which, from
year to year, we trust to be enabled to continue, of the
portraits of those Poets whose names are familiar as
" household words," and whose songs have so often
proved sources of delight and consolation.

London, 13 Bouverie Street,
        Dec. 1, 1860.

INDEX.

Poetical Souvenir.

ALFRED TENNYSON.

ALFRED TENNYSON is the youngest of a poetical triumvirate, and was born in the parsonage of Somersby, near Spilsby, about the year 1810. He was entered at Trinity College, Cambridge, and whilst an undergraduate, wrote a prize poem, also "Poems by Two Brothers," written in conjunction with his brother, and "Poems, chiefly Lyrical," bearing his own name and the date 1830. These early productions, although exhibiting significant tokens of a master spirit, were scarcely sufficient to produce the anticipation of his subsequent triumphs. It was obvious, however, that an original poet had arisen; and that this has been fully realized, the subsequent works of the Poet Laureate sufficiently testify. In 1833 Mr. Tennyson issued another volume, after which he remained silent for nearly nine years. During this period he had not been idle, but carefully pruning his first attempts; and the results of the careful consideration of his earlier writings were given to the world, with other original poems of marvellous power and pathos. In 1847, "The Princess, a Medley," appeared; a remarkable poem, studded with bright thoughts, from which some of the most brilliant of poetic passages in our literature might be quoted. In this volume the Poet Laureate sings some of the

B

sweetest songs in the language. Who does not remember with delight that exquisite little gem,

> " Sweet and low, sweet and low,
> Wind of the western sea," &c. &c. ?

and who has not felt the magnificence of rhythm in the song,

> " Blow, bugle, blow ; set the wild echoes flying " ?

In 1850 appeared " In Memoriam," the most finished of Mr. Tennyson's poems, and one which will endear his name to every heart that has experienced the sorrows of bereavement. It stirs the holiest aspirations and deepest feelings of our nature, whilst its mournful music, like the sobbings of the weird night wind, seems to speak through the darkness of sorrow like the voice of an Angel of Consolation.

Following " In Memoriam," we have received " Maud, and other Poems," " An Ode on the Death of the Duke of Wellington," and " The Idyls of the King ;" the latter containing sufficient to delight the truest lover of poetry, whilst it effectually removes any doubt that might previously have been entertained respecting the pre-eminence of the genius of this great master. Most truly may we endorse the sentiments of one of his most discerning critics —" No poet has within so small a compass exhibited such a wide range of styles and subjects. In his pages, legendary history, fairy fiction, Greek poetry, and trees endowed with human speech, blend in the procession, with Egyptian fanatics, rapt nuns, English ladies, peasant girls, artists, lawyers, farmers,—in fact, a tolerably complete representation of the miscellaneous public of the present day ; whilst the forms vary from fragments of the sublimest epic to the homeliest dialogue, from the simplest utterance of emotion in a song to the highest allegory of a terrible and profound law of life."

We subjoin the following poem, not because it is a fair specimen of his writings, but as being most seasonable at the time our Annual makes its appearance ; and we offer our thanks to Mr. Tennyson for his courtesy in permitting us to make an extract from his " Shorter Poems" :—

THE DEATH OF THE OLD YEAR.

FULL knee-deep lies the winter snow,
And the winter winds are wearily sighing,
Toll ye the church-bell sad and slow,
And tread softly and speak low,
For the old year lies a-dying.
  Old year, you must not die;
  You came to us so readily,
  You lived with us so steadily,
  Old year, you shall not die.

He lieth still; he doth not move;
He will not see the dawn of day,
He hath no other life above,
He gave me a friend, and a true, true love,
And the new year will take 'em away.
  Old year, you must not go;
  So long as you have been with us,
  Such joy as you have seen with us,
  Old year, you shall not go.

He frothed his bumpers to the brim;
A jollier year we shall not see;
But though his eyes are waxing dim,
And though his foes speak ill of him,
He was a friend to me.
  Old year, you shall not die;
  We did so laugh and cry with you,
  I've half a mind to die with you,
  Old year, if you must die.

He was full of joke and jest,
But all his merry quips are o'er.
To see him die, across the waste
His son and heir doth ride post-haste,
But he'll be dead before.

Every one for his own.
The night is starry and cold, my friend,
And the new year, blithe and bold, my friend,
Comes up to take his own.

How hard he breathes! over the snow
I heard just now the crowing cock.
The shadows flicker to and fro;
The cricket chirps; the light burns low;
'Tis nearly twelve o'clock.
.Shake hands before you die,
Old year, we'll dearly rue for you:
What is it we can do for you?
Speak out before you die.

His face is growing sharp and thin;
Alack! our friend is gone.
Close up his eyes; tie up his chin;
Step from the corpse, and let him in
That standeth there alone,
And waiteth at the door.
There's a new foot on the floor, my friend,
There's a new face at the door, my friend
A new face at the door.

FREDERICK TENNYSON.

A BROTHER of the Poet Laureate, who, in a volume entitled "Days and Hours," has given some delightful poems to the world, worthy the name and fame of a Tennyson. That he possesses, in no ordinary degree, poetic capabilities, the following effusions will sufficiently prove; and we trust the time is not far distant when he will fulfil the rich promise of his first volume.

THE BIRTH OF THE YEAR.

LET us speak low, the infant is asleep;
  The frosty hills grow sharp, the day is near,
  And Phosphor with his taper comes to peep
  Into the cradle of the new-born year;
  Hush! the infant is asleep;
  Monarch of the day and night,
  Whisper, yet it is not light,
  The infant is asleep.

Those arms shall crush great serpents ere to-morrow,
  His closed eyes shall wake to laugh and weep;
  His lips shall curl with mirth, and writhe with sorrow,
  And charm up truth and beauty from the deep;
  Softly, softly, let us keep
  Our vigils: visions cross his rest;
  Prophetic pulses stir his breast,
  Although he be asleep.

Now life and death arm'd in his presence wait,
  Genii with lamps are standing at the door;
  Oh, he shall sing sweet songs, he shall relate
  Wonder, and glory, and hopes untold before.
  Murmur memories that may creep
  Into his ears, of eld sublime;
  Let the youngest born of time
  Hear music in his sleep.

Quickly he shall awake, the east is bright,
  And the hot glow of the unrisen sun
  Hath kiss'd his brow with promise of its light,
  His cheek is red with victory to be won.
    Quickly shall our king awake,
    Strong as giants, and arise;
    Sager than the old and wise
    The infant shall awake.

His childhood shall be froward, wild, and thwart:
  His gladness fitful, and his angers blind;
  But tender spirits shall o'ertake his heart,
  Sweet tears and golden moments, bland and kind.
    He shall give delight and take,
    Charm, enchant, dismay, and soothe;
    Raise the dead, and touch with youth;
    Oh, sing that he may wake!

Where is the sword to gird upon his thigh?
  Where is his armour and his laurel crown?
  For he shall be a conqueror ere he die,
  And win him kingdoms wider than his own;
    Like the earthquake he shall shake
    Cities down, and waste like fire;
    Then build them stronger, pile them higher,
    When he shall awake.

In the dark spheres of his unclosed eyes
  The sheeted lightnings lie, and clouded stars,
  That shall glance softly, as in summer skies,
  Or stream o'er thirsty deserts, wing'd with wars:
    For in the pauses of dead hours
    He shall fling his armour off,
    And like a reveller sing and laugh,
    And dance in ladies' bowers.

Ofttimes in his midsummer he shall turn
  To look on the dead blooms with weeping eyes:
  O'er ashes of frail beauty stand and mourn,
  And kiss the bier of stricken hope with sighs.
  Ofttimes, like light of onward seas,
  He shall hail great days to come,
  Or hear the first dread note of doom,
  Like torrents on the breeze.

His manhood shall be blissful and sublime,
  With stormy sorrows, and severest pleasures,
  And his crown'd age upon the top of time
  Shall throne him, great in glories, rich in treasures.
  The sun is up, the day is breaking,
  Sing ye sweetly, draw anear,
  Immortal be the new-born year,
  And blessed be his waking.

TO THE POET.

O GENTLE Poet, whosoe'er thou art,
  Whom God hath gifted with a loving eye,
A sweet and mournful voice, a tender heart,
  Pass by the world, and let it pass thee by;
Be thou to Nature faithful still, and she
Will be for ever faithful unto thee.

Let them disdain thee for thy just disdain:
  Shield thou thy heart against the world accurst,
Where they discourse of joy, and ache with pain,
  And babble of good deeds, and do the worst;
Shed dews of mercy on their wither'd scorn,
And touch their midnight darkness with thy morn.

There blind Ambition barters peace for praise ;
 There Pride ne'er sleeps, nor Hatred waxeth old ;
And dwarfish Folly can his cubit raise
 To godlike stature on a little gold ;
There Madness is a king, and ev'n the wise
Sell truth to simpletons, and live on lies ;

There Pleasure is a sickly meteor-light,
 A star above—a pestilence below :
There Knowledge is a cup of aconite,
 That chills the heart, and makes the pulses slow ;
Remorse, a scorpion's self-destroying sting,
Sorrow, a Winter without hope of Spring.

There Love's clear torch is quench'd as in a tomb,
 Or bound for ever in a golden band
He drags, with eyes fix'd on his early doom,
 Behind lean Avarice with the iron hand :
Fancy, that fill'd the woodlands with his glee,
Scorns at himself, and murmurs to be free.

There Justice, mindless of her holy name,
 Creeps o'er the slime with adder's ears and eyes,
Stirs with dark hand the World-involving flame,
 Thirsteth for tears, and hungers after sighs ;
There Honour is a game to lose or win ;
And Sanctity a softer name for Sin.

For thee 'tis better to remain apart,
 Like one who dwells beneath the forest green,
And listens far off to the beating heart
 Of the wide world, all-seeing, though unseen :
In a cool cavern, on a mountain side,
With rare, sweet flowers, and virgin springs supplied.

Hark thou the voices from the peopled plain
   In tuneful echoes murmuring in thine ears,
Watch thou the sunshine mingle with the rain,
   And mark how gladness interweaves with tears,
And ply thy secret, holy alchemy,
Like God, who gives thee work, when none are by.

And from the twilight of thy solitude
   Note thou the lights and shadows of the sky,
And cast the mighty shapes of Evil and Good
   In perfect moulds of Immortality,
Till they are seen from far, like mountain-light,
That burns on high, when all below is night.

WOMEN AND CHILDREN.

OH ! if no faces were beheld on earth,
But toiling manhood, and repining age,
No welcome eyes of innocence and mirth
To look upon us kindly, who would wage
The gloomy battle for himself alone ?
Or through the dark of the o'erhanging cloud
Look wistfully for light ?   Who would not groan
Beneath his daily task, and weep aloud ?

But little children take us by the hand,
And gaze with trustful cheer into our eyes ;
Patience and fortitude beside us stand
In woman's shape, and waft to heav'n our sighs :
The guiltless child holds back the arm of guilt
Upraised to strike, and woman may atone
With sinless tears for sins of man, and melt
The damning seal when evil deeds are done.

ALEXANDER SMITH.

Mr. ALEXANDER SMITH is one of the most promising of living poets. He was born at Kilmarnock, in the year 1830, and had been employed as a designer of patterns in one of the Glasgow factories; but the publication of his "Life Drama, and other Poems," proved a distinguished success. It was deservedly well received by the public and the press, and gained for the young poet the office of Secretary to the University of Edinburgh. As yet Mr. Smith has not fulfilled the sanguine expectations of his enthusiastic critic, the Rev. George Gilfillan. His poetry, full of original thought and expression, frequently lacks art and regularity; but doubtless this defect, the prevailing fault with young poets, will be overcome by matured judgment and diligent study, for which his present situation is most favourable. In 1857 Mr. Smith published a second volume, entitled "City Poems," and from time to time he has contributed essays and articles to the magazines.

THE POET'S TALE.
FROM THE "LIFE DRAMA."

Walter. 'MONG the green lanes of Kent—green sunny lanes—
Where troops of children shout, and laugh, and play,
And gather daisies, stood an antique home,
Within its orchard, rich with ruddy fruits;
For the full year was laughing in his prime.
Wealth of all flowers grew in that garden green,
And the old porch with its great oaken door
Was smother'd in rose-blooms, while o'er the walls
The honeysuckle clung deliciously.
Before the door there lay a plot of grass,
Snow'd o'er with daisies—flower by all beloved,
And famousest in song—and in the midst,
A carvëd fountain stood, dried up and broken,
On which a peacock perch'd and sunn'd itself;

Beneath, two petted rabbits, snowy white,
Squatted upon the sward.
A row of poplars darkly rose behind,
Around whose tops, and the old-fashion'd vanes,
White pigeons flutter'd, and o'er all was bent .
The mighty sky, with sailing sunny clouds.
One casement was thrown open, and within,
A boy hung o'er a book of poesy,
Silent as planet hanging o'er the sea.
In at the casement open to the noon
Came sweetest garden odours, and the hum—
The drowsy hum—of the rejoicing bees,
Heaven'd in blooms that overclad the walls;
And the cool wind waved in upon his brow,
And stirr'd his curls.   Soft fell the summer night.
Then he arose, and with inspired lips said,—
" Stars! ye are golden-voicëd clarions
To high-aspiring and heroic dooms.
To-night, as I look up unto ye, Stars!
I feel my strength rise to its destiny,
Like a strong eagle to its eyrie soaring.
Who thinks of weakness underneath ye, Stars?
A hum shall be on earth, a name be heard,
An epitaph shall look up proud to God.
Stars! read and listen, it may not be long."
    Violet (leaning over him). I'll see that grand desire
        within your eyes.
Oh, I only see myself!
    Walter.   Violet!
Could you look through my heart as through mine eyes,
You'd find yourself there, too.
    Violet.   Hush, flatterer!
Yet go on with your tale.
    Walter.   Three blue days pass'd,
Full of the sun, loud with a thousand larks;
An evening like a grey child walk'd 'tween each.

'Twas in the quiet of the fourth day's noon,
The boy I speak of slumber'd in the wood.
Like a dropt rose at an oak-root he lay,
A lady bent over him.   He awoke;
She blush'd like sunset, 'mid embarrass'd speech!
A shock of laughter made them friends at once,
And laughter flutter'd through their after-talk,
As darts a bright bird in and out the leaves.
All day he drank her splendid light of eyes;
Nor did they part until the deepening east
'Gan to be sprinkled with the light of eve.
     Violet.   Go on! go on!
     Walter.   June sang herself to death.
They parted in the wood, she very pale;
And he walk'd home the weariest thing on earth.
That night he sat in his unlighted room,
Pale, sad, and solitary, sick at heart,
For he had parted with his dearest friends,
High aspirations, bright dreams golden-wing'd,
Troops of fine fancies that like lambs did play
Amid the sunshine and the virgin dews,
Thick-lying in the green fields of his heart.
Calm thoughts that dwelt like hermits in his soul,
Fair shapes that slept in fancifullest bowers,
Hopes and delight,—he parted with them all.
Link'd hand in hand they went, tears in their eyes,
As faint and beautiful as eyes of flowers,
And now he sat alone with empty soul.
Last night his soul was like a forest, haunted
With pagan shapes; when one nymph slumbering lay,
A sweet dream 'neath her eyelids, her white limbs
Sinking full softly in the violets dim;
When timbrell'd troops rush'd past with branches green:
One in each fountain, rich'd with golden sands,
With her delicious face a moment seen,
And limbs faint-gleaming through their watery veil.

To-night his soul was like that forest old,
When these were reft away, and the wild wind
Running like one distract 'mong their old haunts,
Gold-sanded fountains, and the bladed flags.

[*A pause.*

It is enough to shake one into tears.
A palace full of music was his heart,
An earthquake rent it open to the rain ;
The lovely music died—the bright throngs fled—
Despair came like a foul and grisly beast,
And litter'd in its consecrated rooms.

Nature was leaping like a bacchanal
On the next morn ; beneath its sky-wide sheen,
The boy stood pallid in the rosy porch.
The mad larks bathing in the golden light,
The flowers close-fondled by the impassion'd winds,
The smells that came and went upon the sense,
Like faint waves on a shore, he heeded not ;
He could not look the morning in the eyes.
That singing morn he went forth like a ship ;
Long years have pass'd, and he has not return'd,
Beggar'd or laden, home.

LOVE SONG.

MARY, Mary, sweetest name !
Linked with many a poet's fame.
A Mary, with meek eyes of blue,
And low sweet answers, gently drew
The weary Christ to Bethany,
When no home on earth had He.

When first I saw your tender face,
  Saw you, loved you from afar,
My soul was like forlornest space
  Made sudden happy by a star.
I heard the lark go up to meet the dawn,
  The sun is sinking in the splendid sea;
Through this long day hast thou had one, but one
  Poor thought of me?

O happiest of isles!
  In every garden blows
The large voluptuous-bosomed rose
For musky miles and miles.
I wander round this garden coast;
  I see the glad blue waters run;
In the light of Thy beauty I am lost,
  As the lark is lost in the sun.

O heart! 'twas thine own happiness that gave
  The beauty which has been upon the earth,
  The glory stretching from day's golden birth
Unto his crimson grave.
From thee is every sight;
  From thee the splendour of the firth,
The banquet of the morning light.

Yet, Love, thy very happiness alarms!
  To be beloved is something so divine,
  I dare not hope it can be mine.
My heart is stirring like a nest with young—
  I know that many and many a former brood
Were robbed by cruel fate, and never sung
  Within a summer wood.
Something forebodes me pain;
  The image of my fear—
A maypole standing in the mocking rain
  With garlands torn and sere!

To-day I chanced to pass
  A churchyard covered with forgetful grass ;
And as one puts the hair from off a face,
    I put aside the grass ; and, on the stones,
    Saw roses wreathing bones :
And, in the rankest corner of the place,
Set in a ghastly scroll of skulls and flowers,
And belts of serpents twined and curled,
    I traced a crowned and mantled Death,
Asleep upon a World.
How grim the carver's style—
    The tarnished coffins, rotten palls,
    The weeping of the charnel walls,—
When one is lord of happy hours,
    When one is breathing priceless breath—
Made happy by a smile !

The sheep they leap in golden parks;
    My blood is bliss, my heart is pleasure ;
Then let my song flow like a lark's
    Above his nested treasure.
What care I for the circling cup ?
    What care I for applausive breath ?
For the stern secret folded up
    In the closed hand of Death ?
Bring me Love's honied nightshade ; fill it high ;
    I know its madness, all its wild deceit ;
I know the anguish of the morning sky
    When brain and eyeballs beat.
I cannot throw it down and fly—
    The poison is so sweet
That I must drink and drink, although I die.

A CHILD.

O THOU bright thing, fresh from the hand of God,
The motions of thy dancing limbs are sway'd
By the unceasing music of thy being!
Nearer I seem to God when looking on thee.
'Tis ages since he made his youngest star,
His hand was on thee as 'twere yesterday.
Thou later revelation!   Silver stream,
Breaking with laughter from the lake divine,
Whence all things flow!   O bright and singing babe
What wilt thou be hereafter?

THE SEA.

            THE bridegroom sea
Is toying with the shore, his wedded bride,
And, in the fulness of his marriage joy,
He decorates her tawny brow with shells,
Retires a space, to see how fair she looks,
Then, proud, runs up to kiss her.

CHARLES MACKAY.

No collection of English lyrics would be complete without extracts from the works of Dr. Charles Mackay. Some of his songs are familiar as household worlds in the homes and hearts of the people of England and America. His literary career commenced in the year 1834, by the publication of a small volume of poetry. Shortly afterwards he became connected with the "Morning Herald," and has subsequently been engaged on various literary journals. In later years, his labours have chiefly been devoted to the "Illustrated London News," in the columns of which many of his poems first appeared. At present he is the Editor of the "London Review," a paper which worthily fills a vacant niche in our journalistic literature, and to which he contributes prose and poetical effusions of no ordinary character. His lyrics are certainly amongst the most musical in the language.

HYMN TO PIETY.

O Piety! O heavenly Piety!
She is not rigid as fanatics deem,
But warm as Love, and beautiful as Hope.

Prop of the weak, the crown of humbleness,
The clue of doubt, the eyesight of the blind,
The heavenly robe and garniture of clay!

He that is crown'd with that supernal crown
Is lord and sovereign to himself and Fate,
And angels are his friends and ministers.

Clad in that raiment, ever white and pure,
The wayside mire is harmless to defile,
And rudest storms sweep impotently by.

The pilgrim wandering amid crags and pits,
Supported by that staff shall never fall:—
He smiles at peril, and defies the storm.

c

Shown by that clue, the doubtful path is clear,
The intricate snares and mazes of the world
Are all unlabyrinth'd and bright as day.

Sweet Piety! divinest Piety!
She has a soul capacious as the spheres,
A heart as large as all humanity.

Who to his dwelling takes that visitant,
Has a perpetual solace in all pain,
A friend and comforter in every grief.

The noblest domes, the haughtiest palaces,
That know not her, have ever open gates
Where misery may enter at her will.

But from the threshold of the poorest hut,
Where she sits smiling, sorrow passes by,
And owns the spell that robs her of her sting.

THE CHILD AND THE MOURNERS.

A LITTLE child beneath a tree
Sat and chanted cheerily
A little song, a pleasant song,
Which was—she sang it all day long—
" When the wind blows the blossoms fall:
But a good God reigns over all."

There pass'd a lady by the way,
Moaning in the face of day :
There were tears upon her cheek,
Grief in her heart too great to speak ;
Her husband died but yester-morn,
And left her in the world forlorn.

She stopp'd and listen'd to the child
That look'd to heaven, and singing, smiled ;
And saw not for her own despair,
Another lady, young and fair,
Who, also passing, stopp'd to hear
The infant's anthem ringing clear.

For she but a few sad days before
Had lost the little babe she bore ;
And grief was heavy at her soul
As that sweet memory o'er her stole,
And show'd how bright had been the past,
The present drear and overcast.

And as they stood beneath the tree
Listening, soothed and placidly,
A youth came by, whose sunken eyes
Spake of a load of miseries ;
And he, arrested like the twain,
Stopp'd to listen to the strain.

Death had bow'd the youthful head
Of his bride beloved, his bride unwed :
Her marriage robes were fitted on,
Her fair young face with blushes shone,
When the destroyer smote her low,
And changed the lover's bliss to woe.

And these three listened to the song,
Silver-toned, and sweet, and strong,
Which that child, the livelong day,
Chanted to itself in play :
" When the wind blows the blossoms fall,
But a good God reigns over all."

The widow's lips impulsive moved;
The mother's grief, though unreproved,
Soften'd, as her trembling tongue
Repeated what the infant sung;
And the sad lover, with a start,
Conn'd it over to his heart.

And though the child—if child it were,
And not a seraph sitting there—
Was seen no more, the sorrowing three
Went on their way resignedly,
The song still ringing in their ears—
Was it music of the spheres?

Who shall tell?   They did not know.
But in the midst of deepest woe
The strain recurr'd when sorrow grew,
To warn them, and console them too:
" When the wind blows the blossoms fall,
But a good God reigns over all."

JOHN BROWN.

I've a guinea I can spend, I've a wife and I've a friend,
And a troop of little children at my knee, John Brown;
I've a cottage of my own, with the ivy overgrown,
And a cottage with a view of the sea, John Brown;
I can sit at my door by my shady sycamore,
Large at heart, though of very small estate, John
    Brown;
So come and drain a glass in my arbour as you pass,
And I'll tell you what I love and what I hate, John
    Brown.

I love the song of birds, and the children's early words,
And a loving woman's voice, low and sweet, John
Brown ;
And I hate a false pretence, and the want of common
sense,
And arrogance, and fawning, and deceit, John Brown ;
I love the meadow flowers, and the briar in the bowers,
And I love an open face without guile, John Brown ;
And I hate a selfish knave, and a proud contented
slave,
And a lout who'd rather borrow than he'd toil, John
Brown.

I love a simple song that awakes emotions strong,
And the word of hope that raises him who faints, John
Brown ;
And I hate the constant whine of the foolish who
repine,
And turn their good to evil by complaints, John
Brown ;
But even when I hate, if I seek my garden gate,
And survey the world around me and above, John Brown ;
The hatred flies my mind, and I sigh for human kind,
And excuse the faults of those I cannot love, John
Brown.

So if you like my ways, and the comfort of my days,
I can tell you how I live so unvex'd, John Brown :
I never scorn my health, nor sell my soul for wealth,
Nor destroy one day the pleasures of the next, John
Brown ;
I've parted with my pride, I take the sunny side,
For I've found it worse than folly to be sad, John
Brown ;
I keep my conscience clear, I've a hundred pounds a
year,
And I manage to exist and to be glad, John Brown.

THE MEN OF THE NORTH.

FIERCE as its sunlight, the East may be proud
Of its gay gaudy hues and its sky without cloud;
Mild as its breezes, the beautiful West
May smile like the valleys that dimple its breast;
The South may rejoice in the vine and the palm,
In its groves, where the midnight is sleepy with balm:
   Fair though *they* be,
   There's an isle in the sea,
The home of the brave and the boast of the free!
Hear it, ye lands! let the shout echo forth—
The lords of the world are the Men of the North!

Cold though our seasons, and dull though our skies,
There's a might in our arms and a fire in our eyes;
Dauntless and patient, to dare and to do—
Our watchword is " Duty," our maxim is " Through !"
Winter and storm only nerve us the more,
And chill not the heart, if they creep through the door:
   Strong shall we be
   In our isle of the sea,
The home of the brave and the boast of the free!
Firm as the rocks when the storm flashes forth,
We'll stand in our courage—the Men of the North!

Sunbeams that ripen the olive and vine,
In the face of the slave and the coward may shine;
Roses may blossom where Freedom decays,
And crime be a growth of the Sun's brightest rays.
Scant though the harvest we reap from the soil,
Yet Virtue and Health are the children of Toil:
   Proud let us be
   Of our isle of the sea,
The home of the brave and the boast of the free!
Men with true hearts—let our fame echo forth—
Oh, these are the fruit that we grow in the North!

DIFFERENCES.

THE king can drink the best of wine—
    So can I;
And has enough when he would dine—
    So have I;
And cannot order rain nor shine—
    Nor can I.
Then where's the difference—let me see—
Betwixt my lord the king and me?

Do trusty friends surround his throne
    Night and day?
Or make his interest their own?
    No, not they.
Mine love me for myself alone—
    Bless'd be they!
And that's one difference which I see
Betwixt my lord the king and me.

Do knaves around me lie in wait
    To deceive,
Or fawn and flatter when they hate,
    And would grieve?
Or cruel pomps oppress my state—
    By my leave?
No! Heaven be thank'd! And here you see
More difference 'twixt the king and me!

He has his fools, with jests and quips,
    When he'd play;
He has his armies and his ships—
    Great are they;
But not a child to kiss his lips,
    Well-a-day!
And that's a difference sad to see
Betwixt my lord the king and me.

I wear the cap and he the crown—
    What of that?
I sleep on straw and he on down—
    What of that?
And he's the king, and I'm the clown—
    What of that?
If happy I, and wretched he,
Perhaps the king would change with me!

FAIREST AND DEAREST.

Who shall be fairest?
Who shall be rarest?
Who shall be first in the songs that we sing?
    She who is kindest,
    When fortune is blindest,
Bearing through winter the blooms of the spring;
    Charm of our gladness,
    Friend of our sadness,
Angel of life, when its pleasures take wing!
    She shall be fairest,
    She shall be rarest,
She shall be first in the songs that we sing!

    Who shall be nearest,
    Noblest and dearest,
Named but with honour and pride evermore?
    He, the undaunted,
    Whose banner is planted
On glory's high ramparts and battlements hoar;
    Fearless of danger,
    To falsehood a stranger,
Looking not back while there's duty before!
    He shall be nearest,
    He shall be dearest,
He shall be first in our hearts evermore!

PHILIP JAMES BAILEY.

PHILIP JAMES BAILEY may indeed be justly characterized as the Milton of the nineteenth century. His magnificent poem " Festus " is brimming over with the richest imagery and thought. It has passed through several editions, and is far better known in America than in England. He has subsequently published " The Angel World," " The Mystic," and " The Age, a Colloquial Satire." None of his later works, however, deserve so much attention as " Festus." From it a most delightful volume of " brilliants " might be compiled, and some of the songs scattered through the volume are matchless for music, originality, and chastity of expression. Mr. Bailey was born in Nottingham, in 1816, and educated for the bar; but having deservedly obtained a pension from Government for his poetical excellences, he now devotes his whole attention to the muse.

MIDNIGHT.

FESTUS (*alone*). All things are calm and fair and
   passive, Earth
Looks as if lull'd upon an angel's lap
Into a breathless dewy sleep : so still
That we can only say of things, they be !
The lakelet now, no longer vex'd with gusts,
Replaces on her breast the pictured moon
Pearl'd round with stars. Sweet-imaged scene of time
To come, perchance, when this vain life o'erspent,
Earth may some purer beings' presence bear ;
Mayhap even God may walk among his saints,
In eminence and brightness like yon moon,
Mildly outbeaming all the beads of light
Strung o'er Night's proud dark brow. How strangely
   fair
Yon round still star, which looks half suffering from,

And half rejoicing in, his own strong fire;
Making itself a lonelihood of light,
Like Deity, where'er in Heaven it dwells.
How can the beauty of material things
So win the heart and work upon the mind,
Unless like natured with them? Are great things
And thoughts of the same blood? They have like
    effect.

FIRST LOVE.

WHAT'S worse than falsehood? to deny
The God which is within us, and in all,
Is love? Love hath as many vanities
As charms: and this, perchance, the chief of both :
To make our young hearts break upon the first
And snowlike fall of feeling which overspreads
The bosom of the youthful maiden's mind,
More pure and fair than even its outward type.
If one did thus, was it from vanity?
Or thoughtlessness, or worse? Nay, let it pass.
The beautiful are never desolate;
But some one always loves them—God or man.—
If man abandons, God himself takes them.
And thus it was. She whom I once loved died.
The lightning loathes its cloud—the soul its clay.
Can I forget that hand I took in mine,
Pale as pale violets; that eye, where mind
And matter met alike divine? Oh, no!
Oh! she was fair: her nature once all spring,
And deadly beauty like a maiden sword;
Startlingly beautiful. I see her now!
Whatever thou art, thy soul is in my mind;
Thy shadow hourly lengthens o'er my brain,
And peoples all its pictures with thyself.
Gone, not forgot—pass'd, not lost—thou shalt shine

In heaven like a bright spot in the sun !
She said she wish'd to die, and so she died ;
For cloud-like she pour'd out her love, which was
Her life, to freshen this parch'd heart.   It was thus :
I said we were to part, but she said nothing.
There was no discord—it was music ceased—
Life's thrilling, bounding, bursting joy.   She sat
Like a house-god, her hands fix'd on her knee ;
And her dark hair lay loose and long around her,
Through which her wild bright eye flash'd like a flint.
She spake not, moved not, but she look'd the more,
As if her eye were action, speech, and feeling.
I felt it all; and came and knelt beside her.
The electric touch solved both our souls together.
Then comes the feeling which unmakes, undoes ;
Which tears the sea-like soul up by the roots
And lashes it in scorn against the skies.
Twice did I madly swear to God, hand clench'd,
That not even He nor death should tear her from me.
It is the saddest and the sorest sight,
One's own love weeping ; but why call on God,
But that the feeling of the boundless, bounds
All feeling, as the welkin doth the world ?
It is this which ones us with the whole and God.
Then first we wept ; then closed and clung together !
And my heart shook this building of my breast,
Like a live engine booming up and down.
She fell upon me like a snow-wreath thawing.
Never were bliss and beauty, love and woe,
Ravell'd and twined together into madness,
As in that one wild hour ; to which all else,
The past is but a picture—that alone
Is real, and for ever there in front,
Making a black blank on one side of life
Like a blind eye.   But after that I left her :
And only saw her once again alive.

A LYRIC.

HERE—wear this wreath! no ruder crown
Should deck that dazzling brow.
I crown thee, love; I crown thee, love;
I crown thee queen of me:
And oh! but I am a happy land,
And a loyal land to thee.
I crown thee, love; I crown thee, love;
Thou art queen in thine own right!
Feel! my heart is as 'full as a town of joy;
Look! I have crowded mine eyes with light.
Thou art queen by right divine!
And thy love shall set neither night nor day
O'er this subject heart of mine.
I crown thee, love; I crown thee, love;
Thou art queen by the right of the strong!
And thou didst but win where thou might'st have slain,
Or have bounden in thraldom long.
I crown thee, love; I crown thee, love;
Queen of the brave and free;
For I'm brave to all beauty but thine, my love,
And free to all beauty by thee.

SONG.

For every leaf the loveliest flower
Which beauty sighs for from her bower—
For every star a drop of dew—
For every sun a sky of blue—
For every heart a heart as true!

For every tear by pity shed
Upon a fellow-sufferer's head,

Oh! be a crown of glory given—
Such crowns as saints to gain have striven,
Such crowns as seraphs wear in heaven.

For all who toil at honest fame,
A proud, a pure, a deathless name—
For all who love, who loving bless,
Be life one long, kind, close caress,
Be life all love, all happiness!

HEAVEN.

Is Heaven a place where pearly streams
    Glide over silver sand?
Like childhood's rosy dazzling dreams
    Of some far fairy land?
Is Heaven a clime where diamond dews
    Glitter on fadeless flowers?
And mirth and music ring aloud
    From amaranthine bowers?

Ah, no! not such, not such is Heaven!
    Surpassing far all these;
Such cannot be the guerdon given
    Man's wearied soul to please.
For saint and sinner here below
    Such vain to be have proved;
And the pure spirit will despise
    Whate'er the sense hath loved.

There we shall dwell with Sire and Son,
    And with the mother-maid,
And with the Holy Spirit, one,
    In glory like arrayed;
And not to one created thing
    Shall our embrace be given;
But all our joy shall be in God;
    For only God is Heaven.

RICHARD MONCKTON MILNES.

THIS gentleman, the Member of Parliament for Pontefract, has published four volumes of graceful meditative poetry. He is the eldest son of the late R. P. Milnes, Esq., of Freystone Hall, Yorkshire. In 1831, in his twenty-second year, he took his degree of M.A., at Trinity College, Cambridge. In 1837, he was returned as the representative of Pontefract; and though not a busy politician, frequently intruding his views and prejudices, is nevertheless attentive to his duties, and has materially assisted the cause of social amelioration and reform. We have much pleasure in acknowledging the kindness of Mr. Milnes in permitting the following extracts.

FAMILIAR LOVE.

WE read together, reading the same book,
Our heads bent forward in a half embrace,
So that each shade that either spirit took
Was straight reflected in the other's face :
We read, not silent, nor aloud, but each
Followed the eye that passed the page along,
With a low murmuring sound, that was not speech,
 Yet with so much monotony,
 In its half-slumbering harmony,
 You might not call it song ;
 More like a bee that in the noon rejoices,
Than any customed mood of human voices.
Then if some wayward or disputed sense
Made cease awhile that music, and brought on
A strife of gracious-worded difference,
Too light to hurt our souls dear unison,
We had experience of a blissful state,
In which our powers of thought stood separate,

Each, in its own high freedom, set apart,
But both close folded in one loving heart;
So that we seemed, without conceit, to be
Both one and two in our identity.

We prayed together, praying the same prayer,
But each that prayed did seem to be alone,
And saw the other in a golden air
Poised far away, beneath a vacant throne,
Beckoning the kneeler to arise and sit
Within the glory which encompast it:
And when obeyed, the vision stood beside,
And led the way through the' upper hyaline,
Smiling in beauty tenfold glorified,
Which, while on earth, had seemed enough divine,
The beauty of the Spirit-Bride,
Who guided the rapt Florentine.
The depth of human reason must become
As deep as is the holy human heart,
Ere aught in written phrases can impart
The might and meaning of that extasy
To those low souls, who hold the mystery
Of the' unseen universe for dark and dumb.

But we were mortal still, and when again
We raised our bended knees, I do not say
That our descending spirits felt no pain
To meet the dimness of an earthly day;
Yet not as those disheartened, and the more
Debased, the higher that they rose before,
But, from the exaltation of that hour,
Out of God's choicest treasury, bringing down
New virtue to sustain all ill,—new power
To braid life's thorns into a regal crown,
We pass'd into the outer world, to prove
The strength miraculous of united Love.

THE LONG-AGO.

EYES, which can but ill define
Shapes that rise about and near,
Through the far horizon's line
Stretch a vision free and clear :
Memories, feeble to retrace
Yesterday's immediate flow,
Find a dear familiar face
In each hour of Long-ago.

Follow your majestic train
Down the slopes of old renown,
Knightly forms without disdain,
Sainted heads without a frown ;
Emperors of thought and hand
Congregate a glorious show,
Met from every age and land
In the plains of Long-ago.

As the heart of childhood brings
Something of eternal joy,
From its own unsounded springs,
Such as life can scarce destroy ;
So, remindful of the prime,
Spirits wandering to and fro,
Rest upon the resting time
In the peace of Long-ago.

Youthful Hope's religious fire,
When it burns no longer, leaves
Ashes of impure Desire
On the altars it deceives !
But the light that fills the Past
Sheds a still diviner glow,
Ever farther it is cast
O'er the scenes of Long-ago.

Many a growth of pain and care,
Cumbering all the present hour,
Yields, when once transplanted there,
Healthy fruit or pleasant flower ;
Thoughts that hardly flourish here,
Feelings long have ceased to blow,
Breathe a native atmosphere
In the world of Long-ago.

On that deep-retiring shore
Frequent pearls of beauty lie,
Where the passion-waves of yore
Fiercely beat, and mounted high :
Sorrows that are sorrows still
Lose the bitter taste of woe ;
Nothing's altogether ill
In the griefs of Long-ago.

Tombs where lonely love repines,
Ghastly tenements of tears,
Wear the look of happy shrines
Thro' the golden mists of years :
Death, to those who trust in good,
Vindicates his hardest blow ;
Oh! we would not if we could,
Wake the sleep of Long-ago!

Tho' the doom of swift decay
Shocks the soul where life is strong,
Tho' for frailer hearts the day
Lingers sad and overlong,—
Still the weight will find a leaven,
Still the spoiler's hand is slow,
While the Future has its Heaven,
And the Past its Long-ago.

SONG.

I WANDER'D by the brook-side,
   I wander'd by the mill,
I could not hear the brook flow,
   The noisy wheel was still.
There was no burr of grasshopper,
   No chirp of any bird,
But the beating of my own heart,
   Was all the sound I heard.

I sat beneath the elm tree,
   I watch'd the long, long shade,
And as it grew still longer,
   I did not feel afraid.
For I listen'd for a footfall,
   I listen'd for a word,
But the beating of my own heart,
   Was all the sound I heard.

He came not—no, he came not,
   The night came on alone,
The little stars sat one by one,
   Each on his golden throne;
The evening air past my cheek,
   The leaves above were stirr'd,
But the beating of my own heart,
   Was all the sound I heard.

Fast silent tears were flowing,
   When something stood behind,
A hand was on my shoulder,
   I knew its touch was kind;
It drew me nearer—nearer,
   We did not speak a word,
But the beating of our own hearts
   Was all the sound I heard.

WILLIAM ALLINGHAM.

MR. ALLINGHAM has manifestly caught a fine spirit of inspiration from the most enchanting scenery of Ireland. He is, we believe, a native of Ballyshannon, and proves himself a poet of remarkable promise.

ROBIN REDBREAST.
A CHILD'S SONG.

GOODBYE, goodbye to Summer!
  For Summer's nearly done;
The garden smiling faintly,
  Cool breezes in the sun;
Our thrushes now are silent,
  Our swallows flown away,—
But Robin's here, in coat of brown,
  And scarlet breast-knot gay.
Robin, Robin Redbreast,
  O Robin dear!
Robin sings so sweetly
  In the falling of the year.

Bright yellow, red, and orange,
  The leaves come down in hosts;
The trees are Indian Princes,
  But soon they'll turn to ghosts;
The leathery pears and apples
  Hang russet on the bough;
It's Autumn, Autumn, Autumn late,
  'Twill soon be Winter now.
Robin, Robin Redbreast,
  O Robin dear!
And what will this poor Robin do?
  For pinching days are near.

The fireside for the cricket,
  The wheatstack for the mouse,
When trembling night-winds whistle
  And moan all round the house;
The frosty ways like iron,
  The branches plumed with snow,—
Alas! in Winter dead and dark
  Where can poor Robin go?
Robin, Robin Redbreast,
  O Robin dear!
And a crumb of bread for Robin,
  His little heart to cheer.

ÆOLIAN HARP.

WHAT saith the river to the rushes grey,
  Rushes sadly bending,
  River slowly wending?
Who can tell the whisper'd things they say?
  Youth, and prime, and life, and time,
  For ever, ever fled away!

Cast your wither'd garlands in the stream,
  Low autumnal branches,
  Round the skiff that launches
Wavering downward through the lands of dream.
  Ever, ever fled away!
  This the burden, this the theme.

What saith the river to the rushes grey,
  Rushes sadly bending,
  River slowly wending?
It is near the closing of the day.
Near the night.   Life and light
  For ever, ever fled away!

Draw him tideward down ; but not in haste.
    Mouldering daylight lingers ;
    Night with her cold fingers
Sprinkles moonbeams on the dim sea-waste.
    Ever, ever fled away !
    Vainly cherish'd ! vainly chased !

What saith the river to the rushes grey,
    Rushes sadly bending,
    River slowly wending ?
Where in darkest glooms his bed we lay,
    Up the cave moans the wave,
    For ever, ever, ever fled away !

LADY ALICE.

Now what doth Lady Alice so late on the turret stair,
Without a lamp to light her, but the diamond in her
    hair ;
When every arching passage overflows with shallow
    gloom,
And dreams float through the castle, into every silent
    room ?

She trembles at her footsteps, although they fall so light ;
Through the turret loopholes she sees the wild mid-
    night ;
Broken vapours streaming across the stormy sky ;
Down the empty corridors the blast doth moan and cry.

She steals along a gallery ; she pauses by a door ;
And fast her tears are dropping down upon the oaken
    floor ;
And thrice she seems returning—but thrice she turns
    again :—
Now heavy lie the cloud of sleep on that old father's
    brain !

Oh, well it were that *never* shouldst thou waken from
     thy sleep!
For wherefore should they waken, who waken but to
     weep?
No more, no more beside thy bed doth Peace a vigil keep,
But Woe,—a lion that awaits thy rousing for its leap.

II.

An afternoon of April, no sun appears on high,
But a moist and yellow lustre fills the deepness of the
     sky:
And through the castle-gateway, left empty and forlorn,
Along the leafless avenue an honour'd bier is borne.

They stop.   The long line closes up like some gigantic
     worm;
A shape is standing in the path, a wan and ghost-like
     form,
Which gazes fixedly; nor moves, nor utters any sound;
Then, like a statue built of snow, sinks down upon the
     ground.

And though her clothes are ragged, and though her feet
     are bare,
And though all wild and tangled falls her heavy silk-
     brown hair;
Though from her eyes the brightness, from her cheeks
     the bloom is fled,
They know their Lady Alice, the darling of the dead.

With silence, in her own old room the fainting form
     they lay,
Where all things stand unalter'd since the night she fled
     away:
But who—but who shall bring to life her father from
     the clay?
But who shall give her back again her heart of a
     former day?

THE SAILOR.

A ROMAIC BALLAD.

THOU that hast a daughter
  For one to woo and wed,
Give her to a husband
  With snow upon his head;
Oh, give her to an old man,
  Though little joy it be,
Before the best young sailor
  That sails upon the sea!

How luckless is the sailor
  When sick and like to die;
He sees no tender mother,
  No sweetheart standing by.
Only the captain speaks to him,—
  Stand up, stand up, young man,
And steer the ship to haven,
  As none beside thee can.

Thou sayst to me, "Stand up, stand up;"
  I say to thee, Take hold,
Lift me a little from the deck,
  My hands and feet are cold.
And let my head, I pray thee,
  With handkerchiefs be bound;
There, take my love's gold handkerchief,
  And tie it tightly round.

Now bring the chart, the doleful chart;
  See where these mountains meet—
The clouds are thick around their head,
  The mists around their feet:
Cast anchor here; 'tis deep and safe
  Within the rocky cleft;
The little anchor on the right,
  The great one on the left.

And now to thee, O captain,
　　Most earnestly I pray,
That they may never bury me
　　In church or cloister gray;—
But on the windy sea-beach,
　　At the ending of the land,
All on the surfy sea-beach,
　　Deep down into the sand.

For there will come the sailors,
　　Their voices I shall hear,
And at casting of the anchor
　　The yo-ho loud and clear;
And at hauling of the anchor
　　The yo-ho and the cheer,—
Farewell, my love, for to thy bay
　　I nevermore may steer!

COVENTRY PATMORE.

Mr. Coventry Patmore is the author of a well-known and deservedly appreciated poem, entitled " The Angel in the House," as well as many lyrical effusions of great merit. He has been fortunate in obtaining a literary appointment in the British Museum. The following picturesque and pretty lyrics we extract, by permission, from his writings.

GERALDINE.

Geraldine, the sun is out!
Let us leave this busy rout;
Men and women, girls and boys,
All the city's stir and noise.
Come! and, while we rove along,
I will chant thee such a song!
Song so full of praise, I wist,
'Tis not girlhood's to resist.—
Why do sceptic flittings fine
Wreathe thy red lips, Geraldine?

We are in the fields.   Delight!
Look around!   The bird's-eyes bright;
Pink-tipp'd daisies; sorrel red,
Drooping o'er the lark's green bed;
Oxlips; glazed buttercups,
Out of which the wild bee sups;
See! they dance about thy feet!
Play with, pluck them, little Sweet!
Some affinity divine
Thou hast with them, Geraldine.

Now, sweet wanton, toss them high;
Race about, ye know not why.
Now stand still, from sheer excess
Of exhaustless happiness.

I, meanwhile, on this old gate,
Sit sagely calm, and perhaps relate
Lore of fairies.   Do you know
How they make the mushrooms grow?
Ah! what means that shout of thine?
You can't tell me, Geraldine.

Shall I call thy voice's ringing
Talking, laughing, or wild singing?
April rain through waving trees;
Plashings cool of sunlit seas;
Breezes in the bearded corn;
Robins piping on the thorn;
Prattling brooks in pebbled dells;
Clearest chimes of silver bells;—
None so glad as voice of thine,
Joyous, laughing Geraldine.

Who hath eyes so soft as you—
Such translucent shady blue?
Poets, men of all the earth
Truest judges of true worth,
Steal the life of their sweet books
From the heaven of such looks,
Though Love doom them, every man,
To punishment Promethean.—
Where are those sceptic flittings fine,
That wreathed thy red lips, Geraldine.

THE DESTINED WIFE.

WHEN ripen'd time and chasten'd will
   Have stretch'd and tuned for love's accords
The five-string'd lyre of life, until
   It vibrates with the wind of words;
And " Woman," " Lady," " She," and " Her "
   Are names for perfect, good, and fair,

And unknown maidens, talk'd of, stir
   His thoughts with reverential care ;
He meets, by heavenly chance express,
   His destined wife : some hidden hand
Unveils to him that loveliness
   Which others cannot understand.
No songs of love, no summer dreams
   Did e'er his longing fancy fire
With visions like to this : she seems
   In all things better than desire.
His merits in her presence grow,
   To match the promise in her eyes,
And round her happy footsteps blow
   The authentic airs of Paradise.
For love of her he cannot sleep ;
   Her beauty haunts him all the night ;
It melts his heart, it makes him weep
   For wonder, worship, and delight.

THE MANOR-HOUSE.

It is a venerable place,
   An old ancestral ground,
So wide, the rainbow wholly stands
   Within its lordly bound ;
And all about that large expanse
   A river runneth round.

Upon a rise, where single oaks,
   And clumps of beeches tall,
Drop pleasantly their shade beneath,
   Half-hidden amidst them all,
Resteth in quiet dignity,
   An ancient manor-hall

Around its many gable-ends
  The swallows wheel their flight;
Its huge fantastic weather-vanes
  Look happy in the light;
Its warm face through the foliage gleams,
  A comfortable sight.

The ivy'd turrets seem to love
  The murmur of the bees;
And though this manor-hall hath seen
  The snow of centuries,
How freshly still it stands amid
  Its wealth of swelling trees!

The leafy summer-time is young;
  The yearling lambs are strong;
The sunlight glanceth merrily;
  The trees are full of song;
The plain and polish'd river flows
  Contentedly along.

Beyond the river, bounding all,
  A host of green hills stand,
The manor-rise their central point,
  As cheerful as a band
Of happy children round their chief
  Extended, hand in hand.

Their shadows from the setting sun
  Reach all across the plain;
The guard-hound, in the silent night,
  Stops wrangling with his chain,
To hear, at every burst of barks,
  The hills bark back again.

LILIAN.

SHE could see me coming to her with the vision of the
hawk;
Always hastened on to meet me, heavy passion in her
walk;
Low tones to me grew lower, sweetening so her honey
talk,

Tnat it filled up all my hearing; drown'd the voices of
the birds,
The voices of the breezes, and the voices of the herds;
For to me the lowest ever were the loudest of her
words.

A paleness, as of beauty fainting through its own
excess,
But how discourse of features whose least action could
express
What, while it made them lovely, far surpass'd all
loveliness!

Even when alone together, looks, no utterance can
define,
Mark'd now and then soul-wanderings, that confirm'd
her half divine:
High treasure, ten times treasured for not seeming
wholly mine!

On her face, then and for ever, was the seriousness
within.
Her sweetest smiles (and sweeter did a lover never
win)
Ere half done grew so absent, that they made her fair
cheek thin.

On her face, then and for ever, thoughts unworded used
    to live ;
So that when she whisper'd to me, " Better joy earth
    cannot give "—
Her lips, though shut, continued, " But earth's joy is
    fugitive."

For there a nameless something, though suppressed,
    still spread around ;
The same was on her eyelids if she looked towards the
    ground ;
When she spoke, you knew directly that the same was
    in the sound ;

A fine dissatisfaction, which at no time went away,
But mingled with her laughter, even at its brightest
    play,
Till it touched you like the sunshine in the closing of
    the day.

This still and saint-like beauty, and a difference
    between
Our years (she numbered twenty—mine were scarcely
    then eighteen)
Made my love the blind idolatry which it could not else
    have been.

Her presence was the garden where my soul breathed
    heavenly free,
And lived in naked silence, and felt no perplexity.
When alone with Time I killed him, with a wild and
    headlong glee.

GERALD MASSEY.

IN our last volume we presented our readers with several exquisite lyrical poems by Mr. Gerald Massey, and we again acknowledge, with best thanks, the following contributions; all of which unmistakably bear that stamp of genius which characterizes the writings of this deservedly popular writer. We might in vain seek another passage among the writings of poets, ancient and modern, which might in justice be compared with the following beautiful extract from "The Mother's Broken Idol," a poem of great power and pathos contained in Mr. Massey's last volume, entitled "Craigcrook Castle." We observe that the Messrs. Routledge have just announced a new volume by Mr. Massey, which we anticipate with no ordinary degree of satisfaction.

DEAD!

THIS is a curl of our poor " Splendid's " hair!
A sunny burst of rare and ripe young gold—
A ring of sinless gold that weds two worlds!
Our one thing left with her dear life in it.
Poor Misers! o'er it secretly we sum
Our little savings hoarded up in heaven,—
Our rich love-thoughts heart-hid to doat upon,—
And glimpse our lost heaven in a flood of tears.
A magic ring, through which fond Sorrow reads
Of strange heart-histories, and conjures up
A vanisht face, with its sweet spirit-smiles,
Babe-wonderings, and little tender ways.

At birth her hair was dark as it were dipt
In the death-shadow ; but it rarefied
In radiance as her head rose nigher heaven,
Till she—white Glory!—lookt from a golden midst.
This is her still face as she lay in death!
Spirit-like face! set in a silver cloud,

It comes to us in silent glooms of night;
The wee wan face that gradually withdrew
And darkened into the great cloud of death.

O ye who say, " We have a Child in heaven;"
Who have felt that desolate isolation sharp
Defined in Death's own face; who have stood beside
The Silent River, and stretcht out pleading hands
For some sweet Babe upon the other bank,
That went forth where no human hand might lead,
And left the shut house with no light, no sound,
No answer, when the mourners wail without!
What we have known, ye know, and only know.

She came like April, who with tender grace
Smiles in Earth's face, and sets upon her breast
The bud of all her glory yet to come,
Then bursts in tears, and takes her sorrowful leave.
She brought us Eden just within the space
Of the dear depths of her large, dream-like eyes,
When o'er the vista dropt the death-veil dark.
She only caught three words of human speech:
One for her Mother, one for me, and one
She crowed with, for the fields, and open heaven.
That last she sighed with a sweet farewell pathos
A minute ere she left the house of life,
To come for kisses never any more.

Pale Blossom! how she leaned in love to us!
And how we feared a hand might reach from heaven
To pluck our sweetest flower, our loftiest flower
Of life, that sprang from lowliest root of love!
Some tender trouble in her eyes complained
Of Life's rude stream, as meek Forget-me-nots
Make sweet appeal when winds and waters fret.
And oft she lookt beyond Us with sad eyes,
As for the coming of the Unseen Hand.

We saw, but feared to speak of, her strange beauty,
As some husht Bird that dares not sing i' the night,
Lest lurking foe should find its secret place,
And seize it through the dark. With twin-love's
    strength
All crowded in the softest nestling-touch,
We fenced her round—exchanging silent looks.
We went about the house with listening hearts,
That kept the watch for Danger's stealthiest steps.
Our spirits felt the Shadow ere it fell.

Then the Physician left our door ajar
A moment, and the grim thief Death stole in.
Some Angel passing o'er life's troubled sea,
Had seen our jewel shine celestial pure,
And Death must win it for her bosom pearl.
We stood at Midnight in the Presence dread.
At midnight, when Men die, we strove with Death,
To wrench our jewel from his grasping hand.
Ere the soul loosed from its last ledge of life,
Her little face peered round with anxious eyes,
Then, seeing all the old faces, dropt content.

The mystery dilated in her look,
Which, on the darkening death-ground faintly caught
The likeness of the Angel shining near.
Her passing soul flasht back a glimpse of bliss.
She was a Child no more, but strong and stern
As a mailed Knight that had been grappling Death.
A crown of conquest bound her baby-brow ;
Her little hands could take the heirdom large ;
And all her Childhood's vagrant royalty
Sat staid and calm in some eternal throne.
Love's kiss is sweet, but Death's doth make immortal.

The Mornings came, with glory-garland on,
To deck heaven's azure tent with hangings brave ;

E

Birds, brooks, and bees, were singing in the sun,
Earth's blithe heart breathing bloom into her face,
The flowers all crowding up like Memories
Of lovelier life in some forgotten world,
Or dreams of peace and beauty yet to come.
The soft south-breezes rockt the baby-buds
In fondling arms upon a balmy breast;
And all was gay as universal life
Swam down the stream that glads the City of God.
But we lay dark where Death had struck us down
With that stern blow which made us bleed within,
And bow while the Inevitable went by.

And there our Darling lay in coffined calm;
Beyond the breakers and the moaning now!
And o'er her flowed the white, eternal peace:
The breathing miracle into silence passed:
Never to stretch wee hands, with her dear smile
As soft as light-fall on unfolding flowers;
Never to wake us crying in the night:
Our little hindering thing for ever gone,
In tearful quiet now we might toil on.
All dim the living lustres'motion makes!
No life-dew in the sweet cups of her eyes!
Nought there of our poor " Splendid " but her brow.

A young Immortal came to us disguised,
And in the joy-dance dropt her mask, and fled.

The world went lightly by and heeded not
Our death-white windows blinded to the sun;
The hearts that ached within; the measureless loss;
The Idol broken; our first tryst with Death.
O Life, how strange thy face behind the veil!
And stranger yet will thy strange mystery seem,
When we awake in death and tell our Dream.
'Tis hard to solve the secret of the Sphinx!

We had a little gold Love garnered up,
To bravely robe our Babe: the Mother's half
Was turned to mourning-raiment for her dead:
Mine bought the first land we called ours—Her grave.
We were as treasure-seekers in the earth,
When lo, a death's-head on a sudden stares.

Clad all in spirit-beauty forth she went;
Her budding spring of life in tiny leaf;
Her gracious gold of babe-virginity
Unminted in the image of our world;
Her faint dawn whitened in the perfect day.
Our early wede away went back to God,
Bearing her life-scroll folded, without stain,
And only three words written on it—two
Our names! Ah, may they plead for us in heaven!

LITTLE LILYBELL.

WHEN unseen fingers part the leaves,
 'To show us Beauty's face;
And Earth her breast of glory heaves,
 ' And glows from Spring's embrace:
Flowers Fairy-like on coloured wings
 Float up,—Life's sea doth swell
And flush a world of vernal things,
 Came little Lilybell.

And like a blessed Bird of calm
 Our love's sweet wants she stilled,
Made Passion's fiery wine run balm,—
 Life's glory half fulfilled!
From dappled dawn to twinkling dark,
 Our witching Ariel
Moves thro' our heaven! O, like a lark
 Sings little Lilybell!

And she is fair—ay, very fair!
  With eyes so like the dove;
And lightly leans her world of care
  Upon our arms of love!
It cannot be that ye will break
  The promise-tale ye tell;
Ye will not make such fond hearts ache,
  Our little Lilybell!

As on Life's stream her leaflets spread,
  And tremble in its flow,
We shudder lest the awful Dead
  Pluck at her from below!
Breathe faint and low, ye winds that start;
  O stream, but softly swell;
Your every motion smites the heart
  For little Lilybell!

We tremble lest the Angel Death,
  Who comes to gather flowers
For Paradise, at her sweet breath
  Should fall in love with ours!
O, many a year may come and go,
  Ere from Life's mystic well
Such stream shall flow, such flower shall blow,
  As little Lilybell!

Ah, when her dear heart fills with fears,
  And aches with Love's sweet pain,
And pale cheeks burn thro' happy tears,
  Like red rose in the rain!
I marvel, Sweet, if we shall see
  The sight, and say 'tis well,
When the Beloved calls for thee,
  Our dainty Lilybell!

How rich Love made the lowly sod,
  Where such a flower hath blown!
O Love, we love, and think that God
  Is such a love full-grown!
Dear God! that gave the blessed trust,
  Be near, that all be well;
And morn and eve bedew our dust,
  For love of Lilybell!

———◦◦◦———

THE SQUIRREL HUNT.

IT was Atle of Vermeland
  In winter used to go
A-hunting up in the pine forest,
  With snow-shoes, sledge, and bow.

Soon his Sledge with the soft fine furs
  Was heapt up heavily;
Enough to warm old Winter with,
  And a wealthy man was he.

Just as Atle was turning home,
  He lookt up into a tree;
There sat a merry brown Squirrel that seemed
  To say, "You can't shoot me!"

And it twinkled all over temptingly,
  To the tip of its tail a-curl;
Its humour was arch as the look may be
  Of some would-be-wooed sweet Girl;

That makes the lover follow her, follow her,
  All his heart up-caught,
Until it floats on sleeping wings
  High in the heaven of thought.

He left his Sledge, he bent his bow,
  All day his Arrows rung;
While the Squirrel danced from tree to tree,
  Only himself they stung.

He hunted it into the dark forest
  Till died the last day-gleams;
Then wearily laid him down to rest,
  And hunted it thro' his dreams.

All night fell the sly white snow,
  And covered his snug fur store!
Long, long strained his searching eyes,
  But never found it more.

Home came Atle of Vermeland,
  No Squirrel! no furs for the Mart!
Empty head brought empty hands;
  Both a very full heart.

Many a one hunts the Squirrel,
  In merry or mournful truth,
Until the gathering snows of age
  Cover the treasures of youth.

Deeper into the forest dark
  The Squirrel will dance all day,
Till eyes grow blind and miss their mark,
  And hearts will lose their way.

My Darling! should you ever espy
  This Squirrel in the tree,
With a dancing Devil in his eye,
  Just let that Squirrel be.

THE TWO ROSES.

SOFTLY stept she over the lawn,
        In vesture light and free;
A floating Angel might have drawn
Her hair from heaven in a glory dawn,
        And her voice rang silverly.
Then up she rose on her tiny tiptoes,
Her white hand catches, her fingers close;
You are tall and proud, my dainty Rose!
        But I have you now, said She.

O so lightly over the lawn,
        Step for step went he!
Thinking how, from His hiding-place,
The war of Roses in her face,
        Dear Love would laugh to see!
Two arms suddenly round her he throws,
Two mouths, turning one way, close;
You are tall and proud, my dainty Rose!
        But I have have you now, said He.

————•◦•————

THE FIGHTING TÉMERAIRE TUGGED TO HER LAST BERTH.

IT is a glorious tale to tell
    When nights are long and mirk;
How well she fought our fight, how well
    She did our England's work;
    Our good Ship Témeraire!
    The fighting Témeraire!
She goeth to her last long home,   •
    Our grand old Témeraire.

Bravely over the breezy blue
    They went to do or die;
And proudly on herself she drew
    The Battle's burning eye!

Our good Ship Témeraire !
The fighting Témeraire!
She goeth to her last long home,
Our grand old Témeraire.

Round her the Glory fell in flood,
From Nelson's loving smile,
When, raked with fire, she ran with blood
In England's hour of trial !
Our good Ship Témeraire !
The fighting Témeraire!
She goeth to her last long home,
Our grand old Témeraire.

And when our darling of the Sea
Sank dying on his deck,
With her revenging thunders she
Struck down his foe—a wreck.
Our good Ship Témeraire !
The fighting Témeraire !
She goeth to her last long home,
Our grand old Témeraire.

And when our victory stayed the rout,
And death had stilled the storm,
The gallant Témeraire led out
A prize on either arm :
Our good Ship Témeraire !
The fighting Témeraire !
She goeth to her last long home,
Our grand old Témeraire.

Her day now draweth to its close
With solemn sunset crowned ;
To death her crested beauty bows,
The night is folding round.

Our good Ship Témeraire!
The fighting Témeraire!
She goeth to her last long home,
Our grand old Témeraire.

No more the big heart in her breast
Will heave from wave to wave.
Weary and war-worn, ripe for rest,
She glideth to her grave.
Our good Ship Témeraire!
The fighting Témeraire!
She goeth to her last long home,
Our grand old Témeraire.

Good-bye! good-bye! old Témeraire,
A proud and sad good-bye!
The stalwart spirit that did wear
Your sternness shall not die:
Our good Ship Témeraire!
The fighting Témeraire!
She goeth to her last long home,
Our grand old Témeraire.

Thro' battle-burst and storm of shot
Your banner we shall bear;
And fight for it like those who fought
The good Ship Témeraire!
The fighting Témeraire!
The conquering Témeraire!
She goeth to her last long home,
Our grand old Témeraire.

THE DEATH-RIDE.

SIT stern in your Saddles! grip tighter each blade!
We shall ride down their Guns or thro' blood we shall
    wade,
To-day win a glory that never shall fade;
        Old England for ever, Hurrah!

Oh, the lightning of life! Oh, the thunder of steeds!
Great feelings burn in us like fiery seeds,
Swift to flame out a red fruitage of deeds!
        Old England for ever, Hurrah!

Oh the wild joy of Warriors going to die!
All Sword and all Flame with your brows lifted high;
Ride on, happy band, for your glory swims nigh;
        Old England for ever, Hurrah!

Chariots of fire in the dark of death stand,
To crown all who die for their own dear land.
My God! what a time ere we get hand to hand!
        Old England for ever, Hurrah!

The Sea of Flame wraps us now! take one long breath!
Then plunge for the prize of Immortals beneath.
Silence that Cannonade shouting to Death!
        Old England for ever, Hurrah!

Spring to now! dash thro' now! and cleave crest and
    crown!
For each foe round you strown now a wreath of
    renown!
In a red dash of Sabres ride down, dash them down!
        Old England for ever, Hurrah!

Charge back! once again we must ride the death-ride!
Charge home! smoking hell of Horse, grim, glorified.
You Victor-few, smile in your terrible pride;
        Old England for ever, Hurrah!

Now cheer for the living, now cheer for the dead,
Now cheer for the deed on that hill-side red;
The glory is gathered for England's head.
    Old England for ever, Hurrah!

A LOVER'S FANCY.

SWEET Heaven! I do love a maiden,
Radiant, rare, and beauty-laden:
When she's near me, heaven is round me,
Her dear presence doth so bound me!
I could wring my heart of gladness,
Might it free her lot of sadness!
Give the world, and all that's in it,
Just to press her hand a minute!
Yet she weeteth not I love her;
 Never dare I tell the sweet
Tale, but to the stars above her,
 And the flowers that kiss her feet.

Oh! to live and linger near her,
And in tearful moments cheer her!
I could be a Bird to lighten
Her dear heart,—her sweet eyes brighten:
Or in fragrance, like a blossom,
Give my life up on her bosom!
For my love's withouten measure,
All its pangs are sweetest pleasure;
Yet she weeteth not I love her;
 Never dare I tell the sweet
Tale, but to the stars above her,
 And the flowers that kiss her feet.

THE OLD LAND.

O LEAL high hearts of England,
    The evil days are near ;
When ye, with steel in heart and hand,
    Must strike for all that's dear !
And better tread the bloodiest deck,
    And fieriest field of fame,
Than break the heart and bow the neck,
    And sit in the shadow of shame.
Let Despot, Death, or Devil come,
    United here we stand :
We'll safely guard our Island-Home,
    Or die for the dear old Land.

O, Warriors of Old England,
    You'll hurry to the call ;
And her good ships shall sail the storm,
    With their merry mariners all.
In words she wasteth not her breath,
    But be the trumpet blown,
And in the Battle's dance of death,
    She'll dance the bravest down.
Let Despot, Death, or Devil come,
    United here we stand :
We'll safely guard our Island-Home,
    Or die for the dear old Land.

Success to our dear England,
    When dark days come again ;
And may she rise up glorious
    As the rainbow after rain.
A thousand memories warm us still,
    And, ere the old spirit dies,
The purple of each wold and hill
    From English blood shall rise.

Let Despot, Death, or Devil come,
    United here we stand :
We'll safely guard our Island-Home,
    Or die for the dear old Land.

God strike with our dear England !
    Long may the old land be
The guiding glory of the world,
    The home of the fair and free !
And Ocean on his silver shield
    Uplift our little Isle,
Unvanquisht still by flood or field,
    While the heavens in blessing smile.
Let Despot, Death, or Devil come,
    United here we stand :
We'll safely guard our Island-Home,
    Or die for the dear old Land.

CHARLES SWAIN.

THE name of Charles Swain is always grateful to the true lover of English song. We know of no living poet whose verses are more healthy in tone or exquisitely musical. They not only testify to the author's high appreciation of the beautiful and true, and give evidence of an imaginative, energetic, and accomplished mind, but evince an intense desire on the part of the poet "to do more than write for writing's sake;" and we doubt whether the songs of any writer since Burns have been more successfully useful than those of Charles Swain. We thank him for permission to extract the following, and especially for the contributions to this volume which appear for the first time.

BIRTH-DAY LYRIC.

Down the ladder of Aurora,
When she hath the day before her,
   And the East is clasp'd in gold,
Saw I angels swift descending
With a glory never ending,
   And a majesty untold.
And I whisper'd lowly—slowly—
   Whither tend ye, Angels holy ?
   Spake they forth, " We bring Affection
   To a heart of our selection ;
   To the birthday of a being
   We, afar from heaven seeing,
Loved : and brought by Faith's direction
One pure, priceless gift, Affection !"

Then the scene, like music, fainted,
   Far away in waves of light ;
And a vision like one sainted,
In some old cathedral painted,
   Flash'd its wonder on my sight !

Down a silvery pathway gliding,
In a robe of starry binding,
　　Moved the Presence upon earth :
And I sought my fear to banish,
Lest, in speaking, it might vanish,
　　Saying " Whither ? Angel fair !"
And it whisper'd—soft as air—
　　I bring gifts to one, whose spirit
　　Well deserveth to inherit ;
Friendship, *that departeth never !*
Love, still faithful, fond for ever !
Equal to a life's endurance—
To another world's securance !
So, when Death to heaven may guide her,
Love shall linger still beside her ;
Friendship, mourn o'er days departed,
Nature weep for the true-hearted,
　　Virtue every gift commendeth,
　　May she keep them till life endeth !

Fled my dream ;—for Morn, the singer,
　　O'er my couch her sunbeams held ;
And with touch of golden finger
All my angel-world dispell'd :
Ah, methought, if Love were given
　　Thus—how we should prize its worth—
In its nature all of heaven
　　That might enter aught of earth !
Ah, if Friendship falter'd never,
　　Heart to heart, and thus for ever !

Yet ourselves *within* must find
Charm to gain, and skill to bind ;
Soul must shine ere Friendship's won—
There's no summer without sun !—
Heart must glow ere Love can rest,
And call God's angel to the breast !

THE COTTAGE DOOR.

THE starry silence falls
   Along my sylvan way,
A spirit walks the earth,
   We never meet by day;
And list'ning to the voice
   Of years that are no more;
My feet—Oh! know'st thou why?
   Have wander'd to thy door.

The quiet taper burns
   And makes thy casement bright,
And soft thy shadow falls
   Between me and the light;
I gaze as on a shrine
   My heart would bend before;
My couch had seen no rest,
   Had I not seen thy door.

The Night, as if to breathe,
   Her starry curtain parts;
The very air seems faint
   With breath of lovers' hearts:
Some spirit robes the earth
   In light that heaven wore;
Or is that light thine own?—
   And is that heaven thy door?

BE KIND TO EACH OTHER.

BE kind to each other!—
   The night's coming on,
When friend and when brother
   Perchance may be gone!—

Then 'midst our dejection
  How sweet to have earned
The blest recollection
  Of kindness—*returned!* —

When day hath departed,
  And Memory keeps
Her watch, broken-hearted,
  Where all she loves sleeps!—
Let falsehood assail not,
  Nor envy disprove,—
Let trifles prevail not
  Against those ye love!—

Nor change with to-morrow
  Should fortune take wing;
But the deeper the sorrow
  The closer still cling!—
Oh, be kind to each other!—
  The night's coming on,
When friend and when brother
  Perchance may be gone!

'TWAS COMING FROM THE VILLAGE CHURCH.

'TWAS coming from the Village Church
  I saw my false love nigh,
I said—Oh! shame me not, my heart,
  But let me pass him by.
And so the colour left my cheek,
  The tear forsook mine eye;
And with a timid step, and weak,
  I pass'd my false love by.

F

He look'd—and thought, perchance, to see
  The blush and tear of old ;
But I was cold as he could be—
  That is, I seem'd as cold !
For fast and fast my heart did fill,
  Mine eyes could hold no more,—
He might have seen I lov'd him still,
  Had I not gain'd the door.

I hurried to my own dear room,
  I knelt me down to pray,
But still no firmness could assume,
  My tears they would have way :
Oh ! false, false lips,—oh ! faithless part—
  Oh ! base, unmanly aim—
To seek for years to win a heart,
  Then make its love—its shame !

———◦◇◦———

GIVE ME THE PEOPLE.

SOME love the glow of outward show,
  Some love mere wealth, and try to win it :
The house to me may lowly be,
  If I but like the people in it.
What's all the gold that glitters cold,
  When link'd to hard or haughty feeling ?
Whate'er we're told, the nobler gold
  Is truth of heart and manly dealing !
Then let them seek, whose minds are weak,
  Mere fashion's smile, and try to win it ;
The house to me may lowly be,
  If I but like the people in it !

A lowly roof may give us proof ·
  That lowly flowers are often fairest ;
And trees, whose bark is hard and dark,
  May yield us fruit, and bloom the rarest !

There's worth as sure 'neath garments poor,
  As e'er adorn'd a loftier station;
And minds as just as those, we trust,
  Whose claim is but of wealth's creation!
Then let them seek, whose minds are weak,
  Mere fashion's smile, and try to win it;
The house to me may lowly be,
  If I but like the people in it!

———◦—

TRIPPING DOWN THE FIELD-PATH.

TRIPPING down the field-path,
  Early in the morn,
There I met my own love,
  'Midst the golden corn;
Autumn winds were blowing,
  As in frolic chase,
All her silken ringlets
  Backward from her face;
Little time for speaking
  Had she, for the wind
Bonnet, scarf, or ribbon,
  Ever swept behind.

Still some sweet improvement
  In her beauty shone;
Every graceful movement
  Won me—one by one!
As the breath of Venus
  Seem'd the breeze of morn,
Blowing thus between us,
  'Midst the golden corn.
Little time for wooing
  Had we, for the wind
Still kept on undoing
  What we sought to bind!

Oh ! that autumn morning
　In my heart it beams,
Love's last look adorning
　With its dream of dreams !
Still like waters flowing
　In the ocean shell—
Sounds of breezes blowing
　In my spirit dwell !
Still I see the field-path ;—
　Would that I could see
Her whose graceful beauty
　Lost is now to me !

IMAGINARY EVILS.

LET to-morrow take care of to-morrow,—
　Leave things of the future to fate ;
What's the use to anticipate sorrow ?—
　Life's troubles come never too late !
If to hope overmuch be an error,
　'Tis one that the wise have preferr'd ;
And how often have hearts been in terror
　Of evils that never occurr'd :

Have faith, and thy faith shall sustain thee,—
　Permit not suspicion and.care
With invisible bonds to enchain thee,
　But bear what God gives thee to bear.
By His spirit supported and gladden'd,
　Be ne'er by " forebodings " deterr'd ;
But think how oft hearts have been sadden'd
　By fear of what never occurr'd.

Let to-morrow take care of to-morrow :
　Short and dark as our life may appear,
We may make it still darker by sorrow,—
　Still shorter by folly and fear !

Half our troubles are half our invention,
   And often from blessings conferr'd
Have we shrunk, in the wild apprehension
   Of evils that never occurr'd.

MAIDEN WORTH.

Her home was but a cottage home,
   A simple home and small ;
Yet sweetness and affection made
   It seem a fairy hall :
A little taste, a little care,
   Made humble things appear
As though they were translated there
   From some superior sphere !
Her home was but a cottage home,
   A simple home, and small,
Yet sweetness and affection made
   It seem a fairy hall.

As sweet the home, so sweet the Maid,
   As graceful and as good ;
She seem'd a lily in the shade,
   A violet in the bud !
She had no wealth, but maiden *worth*,—
   A wealth that's little *fame ;*
Yet that's the truest gold of earth—
   The other's but a name !
Her home was but a cottage home,
   A simple home and small,
Yet sweetness and affection made
   It seem a fairy hall.

A cheerfulness of soul, that threw
   A smile o'er every task,
A willingness, that ever flew
   To serve, e'er one could ask !

A something we could wish *our own* ;
     A human floweret, born
To grace in its degree a throne,
     Or any rank adorn !
Her home was but a cottage home,
     A simple home and small,
Yet sweetness and affection made
     It seem a fairy hall !

WHEN THE HEART IS YOUNG.

OH! merry goes the time when the heart is young,
There is nought too high to climb when the heart is young;
     A spirit of delight
     Scatters roses in her flight,
And there's magic in the night when the heart is young.

But weary go the feet when the heart is old,
Time cometh not so sweet when the heart is old;
     From all that smiled and shone,
     There is something lost and gone,
And our friends are few—or none—when the heart is old.

Oh! sparkling are the skies when the heart is young;
There is bliss in beauty's eyes when the heart is young;
     The golden break of day
     Brings gladness in its ray,
And every month is May when the heart is young.

But the sun is setting fast when the heart is old,
And the sky is overcast when the heart is old;
     Life's worn and weary bark
     Lies tossing wild and dark,
And the star hath left Hope's ark when the heart is old.

Yet an angel from its sphere, though the heart be old,
Whispers comfort in our ear, though the heart be old,
    Saying, " Age, from out the tomb,
    Shall immortal youth assume,
And Spring eternal bloom, where no heart is old!"

A SKETCH.

A MAIDEN in the moonlight
    Was sitting all alone :
The shadow of the rose-trees
    Across the green bank thrown :
And, graceful as a lover,
    The quiet moon had placed
A beam, just like a fond arm,
    Around her beauteous waist.

Sometimes with silver finger
    It touched her raven hair ;
Sometimes it sought her bosom,
    As if its heaven were there :
Or glanced from cheek to forehead,
    Or mouth and chin caressed ;
Or silent sank beside her,
    And kissed the ground she pressed.

Some wish they were a fairy,
    But no such wish have I ;
I'd rather be the moonbeam
    My heart's-beloved one nigh !
To chase away the darkness,
    To dwell within her sight,
And, *whilst I lived, to make the world*
    To her a world of light !

HOME AND FRIENDS.

OH, there's a *power* to make each hour
    As sweet as heaven designed it
Nor need we roam to bring it home,
    Though few there be that find it!
We seek too high for things close by,
    And lose what nature found us;
For life hath here no charm so dear
    As Home and Friends around us!

We oft destroy the present joy
    For future hopes—and praise them;
Whilst flowers as sweet bloom at our feet,
    If we'd but stoop to raise them!
For things *afar* still sweetest are
    When youth's bright spell hath bound us;
But soon we're taught that earth had nought
    Like Home and Friends around us!

The friends that speed in time of need,
    When Hope's last reed is shaken,
To show us still, that, come what will,
    We are not quite forsaken :—
Though all were night: if but the light
    Of *Friendship's* altar crown'd us,
'Twould prove the bliss of earth was this—
    Our Home and Friends around us!

MORNING.

O'ER the bending rushes,
    O'er the waving corn,
Where the fountain gushes,
    Speed the wings of Morn;

Like a bird in fleetness,
  Singing on her way—
Fold me in thy sweetness
  Angel light of day!

Flow'rets without number,
  As thy footsteps pass,
Lift their heads from slumber
  Out the dewy grass.
Down the lowly meadow,
  Up the rising ground,
Waves of light and shadow
  Chase each other round.

From the wild bee's humming,
  From the choral throng,
Know we thou art coming,
  Bringing life and song:
Oh! thou golden Morning,
  Brightest boon of earth;
Mead and mount adorning,
  Blessed be thy birth!

IF THOU SPEAK'ST.

IF thou speak'st, though snows surround thee,
  Still the birds believe 'tis Spring;
And with transport flutter round thee
  More to listen than to sing!
If thou smil'st—'tis beauty's summer,
  And thou dost misguide the rose;—
And the lark, the latest comer,
  Heavenward with the mission goes!

If from Nature's golden portal
   Thou bewild'rest nature's own,
How should I, who am but mortal,
   'Scape the witchery of thy tone?
What is Earth if thou forsake it?
   What the seasons unto me?
Earth is what thou deign'st to make it;
   Life is winter without thee!

ROWLAND BROWN.

WE were enabled in our last Volume to make extracts from Rowland Brown's "Songs of Early Spring," and "Lily Leaves," respecting which a reviewer in the "Critic," writes: "No one can deny that Rowland Brown is gifted with a sparkling fancy, and what to him is of inestimable value, the power of investing common objects with uncommon interest." We think the later poems from the same pen, such as "Stones in the Road," "The First Walk Alone," "The Frost Fairy," and others, now published for the first time, are evidences of this power of expressing the poetry of familiar objects. They are, we are requested to add, extracted from MSS. of a volume in contemplation, to be entitled "Fairy-Ring Music," which will contain Idyls and other poems written since the publication of "Lily Leaves."

PRELUDE.

OH! give me Song, and let my weary heart
   Dance to the music of sweet thoughts to-night.
Phantoms of heart and brain, depart, depart,
   And leave my spirit free in its delight.

Oh! give me Song; let its sweet music flow,
   And raise my heart from thoughts of changing things,
Which cast a sombre shade o'er all below
   With the drear darkness of their sable wings.

Spirit of Song, steal gently over me !
Thou angel, whose dear roses are sweet dreams
Fragrant with hopes and blessings yet to be ;
   Light thou the stream of life with love-bright beams.

Raise me from baser thoughts, stir thou my soul,
   Nerve thou the weak till holier trust be given ;
Till I may hear like distant music roll
   God's own voice mingling with the choir of Heaven !

THE ROYAL FEAST.

A CHRISTMAS BALLAD.

KING Christmas held a royal feast,
   And, heedless of the weather,
Though bleak the blast blew from the east,
   His guests all met together.

The wide world was his banquet-hall ;
   And bells from many a steeple,
Like friendly voices, seem'd to call
   Together all the people.

Fond friends from lands afar and near,
   From dark and crowded places,
Came forth to share the monarch's cheer,
   With smiles and happy faces.

His palace walls were richly dight—
   With glorious jewels shining ;
The coral beads of holly bright
   With mistletoe pearls twining.

The board with viands rich was spread
   As the festive hour grew near,
And faster to the banquet sped
   Peasant as well as peer.

Now, at the palace gateway stood
  An Angel clothed in white,
Whose presence filled the multitude
  With tenderest delight.

With smiles did each the Angel greet
  Who knew her sacred mission,
Who felt 'twas she that welcome sweet
  Granted, on *one* condition—

That each should take the token blest,
  That she with blessing proffer'd —
Since none could be a welcome guest
  Who scorn'd the joys she offered !

Brightly the glorious Angel smiled
  (Though not a word was spoken),
Whilst even to the youngest child
  She gave a treasured token.

With joyous thoughts and gladsome voice
  They pass'd the mystic portal ;
Free in the palace to rejoice,
  And share the joys immortal.

And never sweeter sounds did rise,
  Nor eyes more brightly glisten'd ;
For e'en the stars in yon blue skies
  Grew brighter as they listen'd.

But 'midst these happy groups there were
  Unwelcome forms and faces,
On whom the stamp of selfish care
  Had left eternal traces.

Ah ! these appear'd like spectral guests,
  Dark forms of solemn warning :
With hearts, like poison'd scorpion nests—
  They every joy were scorning.

They knew not on that hallow'd ground,
   Heaven seem'd with Earth united,
But sneer'd at those they saw around
   Who love with love requited.

To them the smile of innocence
   Awoke no thrill of pleasure :
No thought of Heaven, howe'er intense,
   Was deem'd by them a treasure.

From blessings heap'd upon the board,
   Their jaundiced eyes turn'd blindly ;
To none, it seem'd, could they afford
   A word of blessing, kindly.

They coldly turn'd from kindness shown,
   No good intention seeing ;
And even the holly seem'd a crown
   Of thorns, to pierce their being !

A curse seem'd resting on their fate ;
   And though no word was spoken,
I knew they enter'd at the gate
   Without the Angel's token.

But when I saw the last of them
   Had from delight departed,
I ask'd the Angel, what bright gem
   She at the gate imparted ?

She said—" I gave the sacred spell
   That binds these hearts together ;
I make them love this feast so well,
   Though wintry be the weather.

" Men call me ' Charity,' who know
   Not yet my home above ;
But there, where I no gifts bestow,
   My Sisters call me, ' Love !' "

" Open this casket: you will find
 The secret gem within it ;
And happy he whose lot it be,
 This festive hour to win it."

I touch'd its secret spring so bright :
 This was the gem, my brother—
A Heart that yearn'd the wrong'd to right,
 And truly loved another !

This heart with nectar fills the cup
 Of life to overflowing,
Blessing the hand that raises up
 The boughs with berries glowing.

Though wild and wintry blew the blast,
 While envious eyes were weeping,
All with this gem, from first to last,
 Were happy Christmas keeping.

To them the joys King Christmas gives
 Shall each year be increased ;
For, oh ! that heart, where'er it lives,
 Makes life a royal feast.

But he who comes with selfish thought,
 For such a scorn'd offender
King Christmas has no pleasure brought,
 And the berries lose their splendour.

Then all who hear the minstrel's song,
 May each, the gem possessing,
Be found their fellow-men among
 With works and words of blessing !

THE FALLING LEAF.

In the cold and drear November,
    I saw a wither'd leaf
Fall from the plume-like branches,
    Like a black tear of grief.
I said, "O Leaf, that thou must go!
I share in this dark hour thy woe."

Methought the Leaf said, "Wherefore grieve?
    What is the cold damp grave to me?
It can but worthlessness receive;
    My spirit lives in yonder tree:
As when to thee a grave is given,
Thy soul will rest in peace in Heaven."

THE FROST FAIRY.

"Oh! look, father! look on the white window pane!
See, see you those flower-like pictures again?
Yes, this seems a garland of daisies to be,
And these like the fringed flowers we found by the sea.
Did the bright angels leave them, who watch'd round
    my bed;
Ere to Heaven they took up the few prayers that I
    said?
Oh! so beautiful are they, so soft, and so light,
I wonder how they could all come in a night!"

"My child, they are beautiful, and you should know,
Though kings could not make them, 'twas God made
    them so.
It matters not though the storm-winds shriek aloud,
And the snow-flakes fall fast from the dark drifting
    cloud;

There's One who looks lovingly down from above,
And the darkness and light are alike to His love ;
And whilst you have slept through the wild wintry
    hours,
He sent the Frost Fairy to sprinkle these flowers."

STONES IN THE ROAD.

ONE day upon a heap of stones,
    A grey-hair'd man was sitting :
With heavy strokes the hammer fell,
    The lumps of granite splitting.
" Old man," said I, " your task seems hard."
    But not to me attending,
" Old man," said I, " 'tis strange this road
    So frequently wants mending."
Then did the old man raise his head,
    And with good-humoured laughter
Said, " Sir, 'twere well if all bad ways,
    Like this, were well look'd after.

" But come, if you are not too proud
    To learn from humble teachers,
I'll tell you now what I have learnt
    From these dumb little preachers.
I know folks, passing every day,
    Will curse the stones I'm breaking ;
And some curse me because they feel
    A momentary shaking.
But 'tis unjust : they do not think
    Of good that is to follow ;
That were the road not rough to-day,
    'Twould not be smooth to-morrow.

" But though they waste their breath and time
　　In vain and foolish clamour,
These stones have given me thoughts as bright
　　As sparks from flint and hammer.
For they have taught me, when I'm sad,
　　And bow'd with care and trouble,
To feel such stones upon the road
　　Will future pleasures double.
And hardest flints the best roads make ;
　　So sorrows the severest
Will often bring the mourning heart
　　To Heaven and God the nearest.

" You'll find, whilst journeying through Life,
　　The roads that are neglected
Will soon become most evil ways,
　　By every plague infected.
Deep ruts with stagnant pools of vice,
　　Springs of affection breaking,
Would ruin all that from the Earth
　　To Heaven is worth the taking.
And Pride, Hypocrisy, and Hate
　　Would pass for sterling metals ;
Whilst all the road of Life would be
　　Choked up with stinging nettles.

" So do not let us pine or fret
　　Whilst Life's rough ways ascending :
He knoweth best, who loveth best,
　　Whilst all our wants attending.
The stones God scatters in our path
　　Should never make us stumble,
But cause us patiently to grow
　　More Christ-like and more humble !
Such stones upon the road of Life,
　　Though fraught with present sorrow,
May make the way seem rough to-day,
　　Which shall be smooth to-morrow."

G

I-LIKE AND I-LOVE.

THERE are two little Fairies who reign on the Earth,
 With spells of all others above ;
We know not their home or the land of their birth,
 But their names are I-Like and I-Love.

So often mistaken in Nature and Fame,
 Alas! they deceive at first sight
The hearts who imagine their blessings the same,
 Or their diadems equally bright!

For I-Like can lay claim to the province alone,
 The mystical realms of the eye ;
But I-Love claims the heart as the *kingdom* his own,
 And all other kings can defy!

I-Like, in his province, the eye, (treach'rous elf!)
 Mocks all who his mandates obey,
Like the will-o'-the-wisp, delighting himself
 In leading his victims astray.

Sometimes he will play the most dangerous freaks,
 Assuming so strange a disguise —
His snares will prove often the daintiest cheeks,
 Ripe lips, and blue beautiful eyes.

And sometimes, may-be, in the heart of a friend
 He may scatter a few pleasant seeds;
But they seldom were known to spring up, or to lend
 The fragrance of beautiful deeds!

For he lacketh the power to win or to wear
 The crown of triumphant success,
And so fickle his fancies and favours appear
 They never can lastingly bless.

But the monarch I-Love, in his kingdom the heart,
 Is changeless in purpose and will,
And blessings his right royal virtues impart
 Are wrought with mysterious skill!

O maiden! who now of sweet orange-flowers dream,
   Beware of I-Like and his wiles;
And breathe not a vow if I-Love, king supreme,
   Reigns not in your heart and your smiles.

FIRST PRAYERS.

A LITTLE boy, who might have seen
   Some Summers six or seven,
On bended knees breathed sweet and low
   A simple prayer to Heaven.

The words had been in infancy
   Taught with a Mother's care;
But though Death took her from the child,
   Death could not take the prayer.

For, as if bending o'er him now,
   The self-same words pray'd he,
" Dear Father and dear Mother bless,
   And take us, God, to Thee!"

But here his little Sister spoke
   (She kiss'd his earnest brow),
And said, " You need not, Brother dear,
   Pray for our Mother now.

" She's gone with angels bright, to dwell
   In realms of endless day;
And, oh! for all that are in Heaven,
   We need no more to pray."

" But," said the little child, who saw
   His Sister's teardrops fall,
' Oh, if I altered what she taught
   I could not pray at all!

" Yet if I must not pray for her
    Each night and morn, I'll pray
That she will ask the King of Heaven
    To take me soon away.

" To take me home to her, where we
    No Death shall ever fear;
For I feel that there are none on Earth
    Who are to me so dear!

" Come, Sister, lay your hand again
    There, softly on my brow;
For I fancy, while 'tis resting there,
    Mother is near me now.

" And do not take the light away,
    But, like she used to tell,
Talk to me of the Angel-world,
    Where she is gone to dwell;

" And smooth my pillow ere I sleep,
    As she once used to do;
For more you seem like her to be
    The more shall I love you."

CELESTA.

PALE beauty of the sunny lands,
Thy form as in my early dreams
        Again I see :
Still with thy prayer-clasp'd lily hands,
Still in thine eyes the sacred beams
        Of life in love for me !

That face which in the sunny spring
(Ere young affection's first eclipse)
　　　Bade Sin depart ;
When, like a touch of angel-wing,
A kiss fell on my thirsting lips,
　　　And Heaven into my heart !

Thou wert to me a star of light ;
A star of God made pure and bright
　　　Thou shinest now.
I feel thy presence in the night,
The angel-halo grandly bright
　　　Upon thy seraph brow !

As in a dream of holy things
In consecrated aisle
　　　From earth above
My soul seems borne on radiant wings ;
For, in the memory of thy smile,
　　　With death I feel in love !

THE FIRST WALK ALONE.

DEAR little Daisy, though not near
　　To watch thy little life unfold,
Yet there's no joy to me more dear
　　Than of thy beauty to be told.
I feel that it must all be true,
　　And long to see thee smile again,
With thy bright eyes, so fairy blue,
　　Unconscious of a tear of pain.
But never deem'd I thoughts so sweet
　　Into my being could have flown,
As when I heard thy tiny feet
　　Had first essay'd to walk alone !

To some the simple act may seem
    A common thing, not worth a thought;
But, as in some ethereal dream,
    Sweet memories the tidings brought.
For I remember'd, darling child,
    Ere I a care of life had known,
How yearn'd I, with ambition wild,
    To make my first essay alone.
No more by loves of home impearl'd,
    No parent's hand my ways to plan,
But self-supporting in the world
    To feel myself indeed a man!

I doubt not, little toddling thing,
    If I a glimpse of thee had caught,
Of failures worth remembering
    I should with grateful heart have thought.
For as a father's eye of love
    Beheld with joy thy first success,
So did my Father, from above
    Look down, my wayward steps to bless,
And, oh! such fairy hopes beguiled—
    My spirit fully understands
The joy that prompted thee, sweet child,
    In infant glee to clap thy hands!

But though it was my boyish pride
    That fill'd with yearning hopes my heart,
That I, with not a whim denied,
    Might act an independent part.
Yet, tired as thou wilt be, sweet one,
    Of thy wee world, the nursery-room—
So scarce my freedom had begun,
    Than other hopes began to bloom.
I felt how weary life would prove,
    Treading its chequer'd path alone;
And first looked up in faith above,
    And ask'd one heart to call mine own.

Sweet innocent, thou know'st no strife
    That haunts the earth which thou hast trod :
Heaven grant, than mine, thy little life,
    May be a closer walk with God !
And when aweary thou shalt grow,
    Needing some heart to lean upon,
May God a heart of truth bestow,
    Worthy the jewel to be won.
And, oh ! sweet child, may Heaven's own flowers
    Of Love upon thy path be cast,
And angels, from celestial bowers,
    Bless, from the first step to the last.

LOVE LETTERS.

As snowdrops come to a wintry world like angels in
    the night,
And we see not the Hand who has sent us them,
    though they give us a strange delight ;
And strong as the dew to freshen the flower or quicken
    the slumbering seed,
Are those little things called " letters of love " to hearts
    that comfort need :
        For alone in the world, 'midst toil and sin,
        These still small voices wake music within.
They come, they come, these letters of love, blessing
    and being blest,
To silence fear with thoughts of cheer, that give to the
    weary rest !

A mother looks out on th' angry sea with a yearning
    heart in vain ;
And a father sits musing over the fire, as he heareth
    the wind and the rain ;

And a sister sits singing a favourite song, unsung for a
    long, long while,
Till it brings the thought, with a tear to her eye, of a
    brother's vanish'd smile;
       And with hearts and eyes more full than all,
       Two lovers look forth for these blessings to fall;
And they come, they come, these letters of love, bless-
    ing and being blest,
To silence fear with thoughts of cheer, that give to the
    weary rest!

Oh! never may we be so lonely in life, so ruin'd and
    lost to love,
That never an olive-branch comes to our ark of home
    from some cherished dove;
And never may we, in happiest hours, or when our
    prayers ascend,
Feel that our hearts have grown too cold for a thought
    on an absent friend;
       For like summer rain to the fainting flowers,
       They are stars to the heart in its darkest hours,
And they come, they come, these letters of love, bless-
    ing and being blest,
To silence fear with thoughts of cheer, that give to the
    weary rest!

UP WITH THE LARK.

One morning awake, in the still daybreak,
    I saw the first sun rays beaming;
And hallow'd light, woke thoughts of delight
    Far better than idle dreaming.
And I saw from its nest, with dewy breast,
    A bird to the blue sky soaring;
And it seem'd each note from its tiny throat
    Was the prayer of Love's outpouring.

But Conscience said, as I lay on my bed,
  " Oh ! why wilt thou take no warning ?
What ! seest thou not what joys are for thee
  When up with the lark in the morning ?

" Why let the Sun's best work be done
  In the fields 'mong the fresh young flowers ?
What ! seest thou not, how precious may be
  The joys of these wasted hours ?
For as the Spring will fragrance bring,
  And tints to the roses fair :
So strength to the weak and health to the cheek
  Is brought by the morning air."
This Conscience said, as I lay on my bed,
  " Wherefore should God be adorning
So early the Earth, if it is not worth
  The first love-thoughts of the morning ?"

Then up with the Lark, if its song has stirr'd
  A single reproach in your bosom :
Be up with the Sun, when the Day has begun,
  To bless the bird and the blossom.
For whilst so simple a thing as a song
  Seems to make e'en the dewdrops gleam brighter,
What ! canst thou not bless, some heart in distress,
  And make thy own burdens grow lighter ?
For happy thou'lt be, if with gratitude free,
  The habits of Indolence scorning,
Thy prayers shall arise to Him in the skies
  Like the Lark to Heaven's gate in the morning !

THE NIGHT.

TO ——.

THIRSTING for Love, as on the parching sand,
   The fainting flow'ret craves a drop of dew—
Like a lone wanderer in a stranger land,
   I yearning sought the beautiful and true ;
Stretching my hands forth in the dreary night,
I pray'd, " O Father, lead me to the Light !"

Darker and deeper still the shadows grew ;
   The wind of Death blew the dear taper out,
That o'er our home a sainted radiance threw,
   And all was dark within and drear without.
And still I pray'd, " Oh, guide my steps aright ;
And lead me, Father, lead me to the Light !"

Amidst the dust and ashes of the street,
   The roll of wheels, the busy rush of life,
I could not hear one chord of music sweet ;
   My heart grew faint and weary of the strife.
With blinding tears still dimmer grew my sight,
Whilst still I cried, " O Father, give me Light !"

No Sister's voice made music in mine ear,
   And lips once kiss'd so tenderly were cold ;
And all torn from me that I held most dear,
   All the bright garlands sweetening days of old.
And every hope seem'd canker'd with a blight,
Whilst I stood yearning for a gleam of Light !

I thought amidst the busy haunts of men
   My soul would soar in music like the lark.
To the stern truth my heart was stranger then—
   How many souls were groping in the dark ;
How many weary yearn'd like mine for Light
Through the dark watches of the silent Night.

But never lips one yearning prayer have said,
　Nor mourner yet one sorrowing tear let fall,
Though like the stricken deer his heart has bled
　Alone in the wild wilderness, but all,
All has been seen and heard by Him whose light
Breaks forth in golden stars to bless the Night.

Such did I feel, thou dear one, when to thee
　God led me like a weary, trusting child ;
A bright star gleam'd across Life's troubled sea,
　A new-found joy my inmost soul beguiled.
I felt a glory dawning strangely bright,
Which made me yearn the more for such sweet Light.

And when God's sun-smile through the chancel gleam'd,
　And even our voices blended in the psalm,
" Nearer to God " indeed my spirit seem'd,
　And like His benediction, a sweet calm
Rested upon my spirit with delight,
And our Heaven-witness seem'd to give me Light!

From all the buried pleasures of the Past,
　Sprang up a sweeter blossom of the heart;
An Angel-hand seem'd on my path to cast
　The brightest roses holy lands impart!
And thoughts that fill'd my spirit grew in light,
As stars that gem the coronet of Night.

God of my life, oh! let this orb of Love
　Herald the dawn of Joy's nativity,
And with its influence, bless'd with thine above,
　Light us through Life into eternity.
And as with deathless stars thou blessest Night
Bless us for ever with serene delight!

MOSS ROSES.

TO ——.

WE know, though all unseen, around us glide
  Spirits we loved with purest of devotion :
We've heard them, when our fears our hopes belied,
  In voice of wind or murmuring waves of Ocean.

We cannot doubt, for oftentimes the voices
  Of our dear guardian Angels seem to speak ;
And when no friendly tongue our heart rejoices,
  Do not they steal the teardrop from the cheek ?

Though their lov'd haunts may be familiar places,
  Yet have we seen them in the loveless street,
With pitying glances and imploring faces,
  And felt our hearts with strange emotions beat.

'Tis past our feeble, poor imagination
  To think how oft they've saved us from the fall
Into some sinful act or dark temptation,
  But when in Heaven, dear one, we shall know all.

And thus if spirits of the pure and holy
  Will come to bless us from the snow-white shroud,
May not the spirits of the flowers so lowly
  Become bright fairies gloriously endow'd ?

If this be so, the spirits of the roses,
  Fragrantly drooping from my vase to-night,
Will heed my voice, and where the Lov'd reposes
  Go forth and minister to her delight.

Linger not longer o'er each fading blossom,
  Emblem of hopes that now can bloom no more ;
But go, and resting lightly on her bosom,
  Tell of sunnier, happier days in store.

Tell her, ye know for fond affection yearning
  One who Life's sweetest solace would impart;
A shrine, wherein the holiest light is burning
  Deep in the secret chambers of the heart.

Tell her such love is fragrant as the roses,
  Sweetening the vistas of the vale of tears,
Which heedless of the spells that Time discloses,
  Shall grow more joyous with the moss of years!

ORANGE-FLOWERS.

TO M. S.

'TIS said, the orange-flowers thou wilt wear,
That from the home of childhood thou wilt pass,
To prove thy chosen *one* heart of the world,
Whose love and peace to thee is all in all.

Go forth, sweet maiden! bud of promise fair,
O'er which in fondness beam'd a mother's eyes,
Watching each leaf of loveliness expand—
Go forth, and blossom as the perfect wife!

Go forth, O blessëd flower of womanhood!
With all the graces virtue calls her own,
And keep their fragrance pure as sanctity,
Wherewith to sweeten ever, heart and home.

Go forth, sweet maiden! as a God-blest bride,
And, for each parting kiss of those beloved,
May from the heart of thy Belov'd spring up
Flowers of affection, fadeless as the stars.

Be Love the guardian angel of thy heart!
In whose bright footprints evermore shall spring
The dearest flowers beneath the eye of God;
And may He lead thee through the paths of peace!

For a fond mother's glance, a sister's voice,
A brother's strong affection, mayst thou find
Concentrated in one true, trusting heart,
All that is felt in heaven and earth by love.

Go forth; and may the blessing of the bard,
And sacred benediction of the priest,
And prayers that fall from lips of those that love,
Be heard, and answer'd by the love of God!

THE LITTLE WIFE.

How strange was the change that came over
    The sorrowful strains of that bard,
Who, only of nature a lover,
    Sought other and sweeter reward!
Till a fairy called Love, in her gladness
    From fairy-land straying one day,
Determined to silence his sadness
    By casting a flower in his way.
Oh! the rose that this beautiful fairy-queen brought
    He yearn'd to his bosom to take;
For she smilingly put in his heart the bright thought,
    " What a dear little wife she will make!"

He calls her his " dear little fairy,"
    Because she such bliss can impart;
Though a Martha at home, she, like Mary,
    Has chosen the far " better part."
'Neath the touch of her snowy-white fingers
    Home blossoms of beauty expand,
Whilst angel-simplicity lingers
    About the sweet works of her hand.
Then oh for the rose that this fairy-queen brought,
    Even earth seems more dear for her sake,
And there's mystical truth in the beautiful thought,
    " What a dear little wife she will make!"

Not only with fairest of faces,
   Not only with daintiest cheek,
Her soul is a garden of graces,
   Of all that is loving and meek !
Draw near her, you cannot help feeling
   The fragrance her virtues impart,
Like sweetest of melodies stealing
   With witching delight o'er the heart.
Then blest be the fairy whose loving hand brought
   Such a beautiful flower for his sake,
And gave to his spirit the magical thought,
   " What a dear little wife she will make !"

SUSPIRIA.

Oh ! let it be that I so live,
   That when beneath the churchyard grass,
   No tongues may whisper as they pass
Aught that in life could sorrow give.

If after death our spirits roam
   The earth, be mine the pleasure sweet
   Of finding flowers I loved to greet
Placed on my grave by friends of home.

Yet if no darling flow'ret wave,
   One wish remains ; 'tis this alone,—
   I would not all that I have done
Be buried with me in the grave.

My Songs, ah ! be they, as I trust,
   Forget-me-nots in many a heart,
   Some sweeten'd solace to impart,
When he who sings sleeps in the dust.

S. H. BRADBURY.

AMONG the poets of the present, perhaps there are few who have so well sustained their reputation, or whose sweet snatches of song have become so generally admired as those of Mr. S. H. Bradbury, who, under the *nom de plume* of " Quallon," has written some of the most musical lyrics in the language. He is of humble parentage, a native of Nottingham, and, like all other poets of the people, his career has been most remarkable. In October, 1857, the Government conferred upon him a pension of 50*l.* His writings have been most favourably received by the reviewers. They are distinguished by much elegance and beauty of simile, and a musical charm of a very high order. The following beautiful poem, entitled " Little Mary," was very highly commended by the " critic " of the " Times." We acknowledge the receipt of a copy of a charming volume, entitled " Leoline " (London: Hall, Virtue, and Co.), from which we have made a few extracts. The volume exhibits a joyous perception of the beauties of nature, thought, spirit, and the true poetic fire. We thank Mr. Bradbury, also, for his original contributions to our pages.

LITTLE MARY.

LITTLE Mary comes to greet me
　　With a smile almost divine ;
And her looks like pleasures meet me,
　　As she lays her hand in mine.
Fairest creature ! ever straying,
　　With a grace as light as day ;
Like a lamb with sunbeams playing,
　　In the perfumed hours of May.

Then she asks me if I love her,
　　And her little auburn curls
Fall in clusters, and half cover
　　Her sweet lips, enriched with pearls.

Then she smiles with grace so simple—
    Half akin to Heaven she seems;
Love plays round each moulded dimple,
    Like a fairy in day-dreams.

'Gainst no household duties sinning,
    With a seraph's voice she talks;
And the kindest praises winning,
    Makes a Heaven where she walks.
And at night to the Eternal
    Whispers forth her fondest prayer;
With her presence home is vernal,
    Something like an angel'd sphere.

Then she twines her arms around me,
    Tells me how she learns to spell;
Till a power unseen has bound me,
    Far too pure for tongue to tell.
Earthly grossness comes not near her,
    Charms divine her ways imbue;
O ye watchful angels spare her,
    Guide her to the pure and true.

Quick and graceful as a fairy,
    Type of what the lovely are;
Perfect is the form of Mary,
    ' Rayed with beauty like a star.
And endowed with all the graces,
    Which the Pleading Angel gives;
I can see by outward traces,
    That the flower of Eden lives.

And her anxious eyes will glisten
    As she hears my footsteps near:
Oft to her sweet voice I listen,
    Then home seems a music-sphere

11

And her gambols ever teach me
  Pleasure is not always vain ;
Angel-touches seem to reach me—
  Then I feel a child again.

Then she tells me some bright story
  Of the little feats she's done,
How she learnt the Saviour's glory,
  How the prize at school she won.
And thus she talks through evening hours
  With an air of sweet delight;
Then with lips pressed to her flowers,
  Breathes the tender words, " Good night."

----◆----

TO ——.

FROM " EDENOR:" A DRAMATIC POEM OF GREAT POWER AND
PATHOS.

I WALKED with thee one wealthy summer's night,
  In grove bedecked with flowers ;
Our cheeks embathëd in the moon's pale light,
  Falling in beamy showers.
There was a luxury in thy silken hair
  When rippling o'er thy cheek
In radiant waves; thine eyes threw light so fair,
  I felt too great to speak.

My soul danced high in bliss—a splendid swoon—
  A brilliant rapture swept
High up my heart, clear as the silent moon,
  And stars their splendours wept.
I heard the beatings of thine heart, and felt ;
  Cold dew-drops chill'd thy breast ;
And saw the distant hills of white clouds melt
  Far down the star-paved west.

The azure gulf of Heaven was filled with stars,
　The glittering fruit of God ;
The mellowed moonbeams fell like golden bars,
　Gilding Earth's dew-bathed sod.
I saw thy languaged eyes were ripe with charms,
　A summer-burst of love ;
And close insph, red in thy pale round arms,
　I dream'd I shone above.

I felt thee clasp me and impart a thrill
　Of sweet, delicious pain ;
I woke, and saw night's blazing stars were still
　Glass'd in the slumbering main.
Thy feet were buried in a bank of moss,
　Enrich'd with night's cool tears ;
The moon grew blind with clouds—we felt its loss,
　And watched the panting spheres.

THE VILLAGE CHURCH.

NEAR the village church I wander
　When the daylight dies away ;
When the sunset on the windows
　Lingers with a parting ray ;
Throwing on the floor a radiance,
　Rose-light streaked with golden bars,
Tints of amethyst and violet,
　As though showered from the stars.

And so tranquil in the evening
　Looks that temple quaint and hoar,
That I'm led to muse in silence
　On the friends I see no more ;—
Walk beside the graves of kindred
　Whom I loved in earliest years ;
Whose long loss Time cannot darken,
　While their memories rise in tears.

Oft I've paused by night and wondered
  On the stillness all around;
Seen the old church spire by moonlight
  Cast its shadow on the ground,—
Lying on the graves where daisies
  Half revealed their crimson rims
Dipped in dewdrops; where Night's glory,
  Tremulous and star-flushed, swims.

And those dewdrops oft I've fancied
  Were the tears by angels shed,
For the loss of mortals fallen
  Untimely among the dead.
For the Night is full of mystery,
  And we know not when alone,
How nearly the dead one's spirit
  Past the living form has flown.

To that village church I'm wedded,
  Where the ivy springs and falls,—
For the solemn reign of centuries,
  Carved upon its crumbling walls.
By the scene I'm taught how mortals,
  Filled with thought may look afar,
And behold, through death, the portals
  Where God's pale immortals are.

GERALDINE.

Most stately was the splendid Geraldine,
  A picture perfect as she lay asleep;
A brow where glorious intellect was seen,
  Where artist might new thoughts of beauty reap.
Arms white as marble, and so sweetly round,
  Bare on the silken coverlet were laid;
Like image of snow-wreaths in lakelet drowned,
  And hushed in dreams her lips like rose-leaves played!

The faintest pink dwelt on each rounded cheek,
  And to the pillow gave a rosy hue,
Like morn's faint blush on lilies; eyes might seek
  Its like in crimson tulip filled with dew.
A band of blushing velvet bound each arm,
  With diamonds sprinkled, raining sparks of light;
Each violet-coloured vein ran like a charm,
  Till all were lost 'mong curls dark as the night!

Her bosom wave-like ever rose and fell,
  The coverlet revealed its ample mould;
White clouds ne'er looked so fair seen from a dell,
  Nor lovelier figure could these eyes behold.
And when the morning thro' her chamber blushed,
  It seemed to borrow beauty as it strayed
To where she lay in gleaming visions hushed,
  Still as a goddess in a robe arrayed.

And when she rose she bared her beauteous form,
  And in the water plunged while ripples prest,
In hurried crowds, to dally and to warm,
  To clasp and lie upon her heaving breast.
She rises from the bath; in silken dress,
  Made loose and lustrous soon her form appears;
While in a sable mass each glossy tress,
  Holds in its fragrant coil pearls pale as tears.

With rarest majesty she walks the floor,
  In honied accents warbles some sweet strain,
By olden bard, full of romantic lore,
  With lucent fancies lit like drops of rain!
A full midnight of glory gleams her eye,
  Where the attracted sunlight swarms and wades;
And every zephyr, ere it flutters by,
  Her silken bodice lovingly invades.

Then to her bower she walks with cherished book,
    Whose leaves are perfumed and whose thoughts are
        rare;
E'en there stray sunbeams thro' the vine-leaves look,
    As though they strove to find an angel there!
More wealth of beauty never touched the earth,
    Such wondrous eyes before were never seen;
No eloquence could ever paint the worth
    Of the affluent-hearted Geraldine!

I KNOW A COT.

I KNOW a cot where sweetly dwells
    A maiden I'll not name ;
Whose voice is rich as gold-tongued bells,—
    More unto me than fame.
A woodbine climbs about the door,
    As though it loved the scene,
And clung there only to adore
    My bashful maiden queen.

Round that dear cot in dreams by night
    My fancies love to roam ;
For Love burns with undying light
    About its idol's home.
It makes an Eden where it flowers,
    And from the heart it springs,
Chants like the lark in summer hours,
    Till earth with music rings.

I see this maiden in the morn,
    A blush upon her face,
Pale as a wild rose newly born
    In some calm, sunny place.

And oh! the brightness of her eye
  Bewitches and endears;
'Tis dazzling as an azure sky,
  Shines like a violet's tears!

I dare not speak or I would say
  How wildly throbs this heart,
Unclasped and opened to her sway,
  Like blossoms when they part.
And thus it is, the charm that gives
  Enchantment leads us on
To love, and when no more it lives,
  We mourn the beauty gone.

WHAT SHALL I DO TO WIN HER HAND?

WHAT shall I do to win her hand?
  I've tried all things in vain;
I've vowed by all things in the land,
  The open sky and plain.
I've told her that my love is deep,
  That idle dreams have past;
That this lone memory will keep
  Her form while life shall last.

She heeds me not but turns away,
  A sweet smile in her look,
As beautiful as bloom of May
  On leaves of gilded book;
Her charms unclosing one by one,
  Whene'er she moves or speaks,
While coral hues lie dreaming on
  Her round and peerless cheeks.

In every step there is a grace
    That words could never tell,
Where gleams of Paradise I trace,
    And beauty's luring spell.
All beauty has a power supreme,
    A thrill that never tires,
It clasps and crowns each happy dream,
    And love's emotion fires.

What must I do to win her hand?
    How shall I fondly plead?
Like blinding sparks of gold in sand,
    Her glances heavenward lead.
The chords of this poor heart she thrills,
    I'm bound in slavery's chain,
I've sought her by the lakes and rills,
    But sought and wooed in vain!

THE NOBLEMAN OF EARTH.

THE truest nobleman of earth
    Is he who loves to be
The first companion of the good,
    The hero of the free!
Who works undaunted for the poor,
    Who sees no rank in names;
Whose hopes ascend to Heaven in crowds,
    As sparks fly up from flames!

Give me that nobleman of mind
    Who loves a noble cause;
The right of Labour's sturdy sons,
    And Freedom's righteous laws!
The hater of each evil scheme
    A tyrant may advance;
A giant's strength about his heart,
    Thoughts brilliant in his glance.

I love the nobleman of Earth
　Who strives to bless the age,
And leaves a glory that is caught
　On history's faithful page !
Whose name the millions love to lisp,
　Truth's sure unflinching guest ;
Who shines in love as does the sun
　In palace of the west.

He's deathless as the mighty skies,
　When jewelled through with stars ;
Can feel God's beauty in a blaze
　Burst through his prison bars.
No mandate from the tyrant breaks
　His spirit's upward bound ;
While high in every liberal creed
　His name is blazoned round !

And perjured kings may pass from earth,
　Their pomp and lustre fade ;
But Nature's nobleman unclasps
　The cruel laws they've made.
His worshipp'd monarch is his God,
　He leaves a name behind,
Flush'd with effulgence that reflects
　His majesty of mind.

THE DREAMER.

Upon a couch the maiden lay,
　Hush'd in a realm of silver dreams ;
And o'er her head shook lemon bloom,
　And at her feet ran tiny streams.
One arm lay naked on the couch,
　So warm and beautiful and white ;
So fair 'twould not one shade have cast
　Though in the midst of sunniest light.

Her cheeks had but the faintest pink,
  Like cloud-blush on pure marble laid;
While brilliant fancies on her mind,
  Like loving birds in blossoms played!
The tulip's glow bloom'd through her lips—
  Love's fragrant portals half apart;
A sculptor might have learnt from her
  A secret to perfect his art.

Her eyes were closed, and on the lids
  The azure veins seemed pleased to dwell;
While o'er one cheek in ebony crowds
  Her curls in odorous luxury fell.
Her breathing was as low and sweet
  As zephyrs 'round an eglantine;
A rich faint smile played on her face
  Like diamond's fire on rosy wine.

One cheek was in the pillow hid,
  Her peerless brow ungemm'd, unbound;
Two radiant rings of palest gold
  In splendour clasp'd each white arm round.
She lay hush'd in the land of dreams,
  Sweet land I'd ever hover near;
Land where the cares of life are lost,
  And where the paths of Heaven appear.

JOHN CRITCHLEY PRINCE.

A CORRESPONDENT has sent us the accompanying acceptable contributions from John Critchley Prince, a working man, but, nevertheless, a true poet. We understand that, through illness and misfortune, the circumstances of Mr. Prince are such that he has been compelled to seek charitable assistance in order to obtain the necessary means of support. Should any of our readers, in distributing their Christmas bounty, be desirous of lending their aid, we shall be happy to give them the poet's address.

***

NOTHING IS LOST.

NOTHING is lost; the drop of dew
    That trembles on the leaf or flower
Is but exhaled, to fall anew
    In summer's thunder shower;
Perchance to shine within the bow
    That fronts the sun at fall of day;
Perchance to sparkle in the flow
    Of fountains far away.

Nought lost; for even the tiniest seed,
    By wild birds borne on breezes blown,
Finds something suited to its need,
    Wherein 'tis sown and grown;
Perchance finds sustenance and soil
    In some remote and desert place,
Or 'mid the crowded homes of toil
    Sheds usefulness and grace.

The little drift of common dust,
    By the March winds disturbed and tossed,
Though scattered by the fitful gust,
    Is changed, but never lost;

It yet may bear some fruitful stem,
  Some proud oak battling with the blast,
Or crown with verdurous diadem
  Some ruin of the past.

The furnace quenched, the flame put out,
  Still cling to earth or soar in air,
Transformed, diffused, and blown about,
  To burn again elsewhere;
Haply to make the beacon-blaze
  That gleams athwart the briny waste,
Or light the social lamp, whose rays
  Illume the home of taste.

The touching tones of minstrel art,
  The breathings of some mournful flute,
Which we have heard with listening heart,
  Are not extinct when mute;
The language of some household song,
  The perfume of some cherished flower,
Though gone from outward sense, belong
  To memory's after hour.

So with our words, or harsh or kind,
  Uttered, they are not all forgot,
But leave some trace upon the mind,
  Pass on, but perish not;
As they are spoken, so they fall
  Upon the spirit spoken to,
Scorch it like drops of burning gall,
  Or soothe like honey-dew.

So with our deeds, for good or ill
  They have their power, scarce understood,
Then let us use our better will
  To make them rife with good.

Like circles on a lake they go,
    Ring within ring, and never stay;
Oh, that our deeds were fashioned so
    That they might bless alway!

Then, since these lesser things ne'er die,
    But work beyond our poor control,
Say, shall that suppliant for the sky
    The greater human soul?
Ah, no! it still will spurn the past,
    And seek the future for its rest,
Joyful! if it be found at last
    'Mong the redeemed and blest.

THE DARKEST HOUR.

DESPAIR not, Poet, whose warm soul aspires
    To breathe the exalted atmosphere of fame;
Give thy heart words, but purify its fires,
    So that thy song may consecrate thy name!
Sing on and hope, nor murmur that the crowd
    Are slow to hear and recognize thy lay;
Thy time will come, if thou art well endowed:
    The darkest hour is on the verge of day.

Despair not, Genius, wheresoe'er thou art,
    Whate'er the bent and purpose of thy mind;
Use thy great gifts with an unfailing heart,
    And wait till fortune deigneth to be kind;
The world is tardy in its help and praise,
    And doubts and dangers may obstruct thy way,
But light oft pierces through the heaviest haze:
    The darkest hour is on the verge of day.

Despair not, Patriot, who in dreams sublime
  See'st for thy country glories yet unborn,
And fain wouldst chide the laggard wings of Time,
  Because they bring not the transcendent morn;
Be firm in thy devotion, year by year
  We seem to travel on a sunward way,
And what is dubious now may yet be clear:
  The darkest hour is on the verge of day.

Despair not, Virtue, who in sorrow's hour
  Sigh'st to behold some idol overthrown,
And from the shade of thy domestic bower
  Some green branch gone, some bird of promise flown.
God chastens but to prove thy faithfulness,
  And in thy weakness He will be thy stay;
Trust and deserve, and He will soothe and bless:
  The darkest hour is on the verge of day.

Despair not, Man, however low thy state,
  Nor scorn small blessings that around thee fall;
Learn to disdain the impious creed of Fate,
  And own the Providence who governs all.
If thou art baffled in thy earnest will,
  Thy conscience clear, thy reason not astray,
Be this thy faith and consolation still—
  The darkest hour is on the verge of day.

THOMAS COX.

THE poems contributed to our last volume by this esteemed author were, as they well deserved to be, most favourably received, and justifies us in endorsing the opinion of one of his reviewers, that he possesses imaginative power and strength of expression of no mean order.

_____

THE HERMIT.

ON yonder lonely Island,
    Where the green alders grow,
A mouldering pile with ivy clad
    Frowns on the waves below.
It is a pleasant sight, they say,
    When summer days are done,
To see thro' the old battlements
    The setting of the sun.

In times gone by, in time of old,
    Ere ruin crept the walls,
Fierce warrior's tramp and battle's shout
    Resounded through its halls.
And on those hills, those barren hills,
    We see so far away,
There was a bloody battle fought
    Upon some luckless day.
For often by the pale moonlight
    Rude peasants with their spades,
Grim, ghostly skulls are turning up
    With broken shields and blades.

Now, once upon a winter's day,
    When forest trees were brown,
I ask'd a little Fisher-boy
    To row me up and down.

A pilgrim stood upon the hill,
   And look'd into the west,
His beard, that was so very white,
   Hung half way down his breast.

" I see him," said the little boy,
   " When a mist comes from the land,
Far down the west to cast a look,
   Then wave his bony hand.
And as I'm veering to and fro,
   Just in the dusk of night,
I often look across the wave
   To see the old man's light.

" When the wild wind shakes the ivy
   Upon the ruins old,
He roams about the grey-grown towers
   That look so damp and cold.
Then as the wintry sun goes down,
   And the night breeze rocks the tree,
I hear him sing his even song
   Across the dusky sea."

SONG.

" When winter from his dreary land
   Locks up the streams around,
I love to see the white, white snow,
   Fall softly to the ground.
I love to see the white, white snow,
   Fall on the narrow sea,
That ever-rolling watery belt
   Which shuts the world from me.

" Against the cold, cold wintry blasts
   I close my rustic door,
When howling by the leafless trees
   They sweep the sandy shore.

Upon the sandy shore there beat
    The billows of that sea,
That ever-rolling watery belt
    Which shuts the world from me.

" 'Tis said this life is but a dream,
    So soon it fades way;
My life; ah, me! what has it been
    But a short April day?
Sometimes 'twas rough, sometimes 'twas smooth,
    Yes, like the changeful sea,
That ever-rolling watery belt
    Which shuts the world from me."

MAY MORNING.

Now Aurora's just appearing
    From the hills afar;
In the east I see her leering
    From her grey, cold car.
And the earth throws off its sorrow
    At the approach of day;
And darkness, like the dew-drops,
    Silently steals away.

Hark! there comes a lusty cheer
    From the straw-capp'd shed;
'Tis the song of chanticleer
    Rising from his bed.
Now he calls the merry ploughman
    Forth into the fields,
When the morn in all its freshness
    Health and pleasure yields.

I

Hearts long chill'd by winter's cold
    Melt with the snow ;
The river bursts its icy fold,
    Again the ripples flow.
Echoing through the meadow-land,
    Sweet their voices ring,
Cheering every drooping heart
    With a glow of spring.

Sunshine from the south is call'd,
    Once more the sky is blue,
And trees so long in sorrow bald
    Again their leaves renew.
Thus the earth throws off its sadness
    In the merry May,
So let us throw off all winter,
    And be glad and gay.

THE MERRY MONARCH.

Cold blows the wind across the moor,
    Piercingly blows the wintry wind;
The snow comes pattering 'gainst the door,
    And naught of summer lurks behind.
The brooks have ceased their pleasant hum,
And birds upon the boughs are dumb.

But at this dull and dreary time
    There always comes a welcome guest :
What tho' his beard be fringed with rime,
    His heart beats warmly in his breast,
And by the social hearth can be
The best and gayest company.

No lark goes up from flowery lawn
  To greet the sun through misty cloud,
Tho' spring-time and its mirth are gone,
  And nature dons its wintry shroud,
We still find pleasure with our friend
Just as the old year nears his end.

When near his end, the aged year,
  We welcome in the good old King,
We treat him with the best of cheer,
  And at his feet our dainties fling.
What time the bitter winds do blow
The bells ring welcome cross the snow.

The while the great world sleeps and wakes,
  And Christmas doth his visits pay,
Old Time still on his journey takes,
  And comrades yearly pass away.
Then know, my good old hearty friend,
Our meetings here must have an end.

THE ROSE.

In my garden grows
        The rose.
Sweet summer flower,
Queen of beauty's bower,
How fresh at morning's hour
        Is the rose!

Like a modest maiden,
Once her breast was laden
In the early morning with the dew;
Young Zephyr chanc'd to sally
Forth from his pleasant valley
That merry, merry morn, her charms to view.
Said he, "Oh, fairest gem
In Flora's diadem!"
Which brought upon her face the crimson hue.

Some have made their pet
                The violet:
I quite agree with them, .
It is a pretty gem,
I will not, then, condemn
                The violet.

But what can e'er disclose
Such fragrance as the rose,
                Sweet rose!
Queen of beauty's bower,
Caress'd by breeze and shower,
England's adopted flower,
                The bonnie rose!

THE SNOWDROP.

While the tardy spring
                Is slumbering
Far, far away in arbours green,
                The snowdrop's seen
Up from its lowly bed thro' damp moss peeping.
With joy we see appear
The first flower of the year,
Thrice welcome are ye here,
What time the primrose in the mould is sleeping.

When winter looketh down,
                With angry frown,
Upon your innocent breast,
                Be at rest,
Sweet flower of hope! and on thy sire's retreating,
To his northern gloom,
Rise from thy snowy tomb,
Herald of bud and bloom,
And give the new-born year a merry greeting.

CAROLINE GIFFARD PHILLIPSON.

IN our last volume we published several of the beautiful effusions of this accomplished writer, which were highly commended by the reviewers, and quoted in several publications. The following strikingly original and expressive poems are here published for the first time, with the exception of an extract from the author's delightful poetic romance entitled " Eva."

THE CHURCHYARD GRAVE.

By a low and grassy mound
   In the village churchyard still,
Where the dark yews wav'd around
   Under shelter of the hill ;

Where the ivy-mantled church
   Seem'd like guardian spirit keeping
With its snug and antique porch
   O'er the rest-place of the sleeping ;

Sat a little rustic maiden
   With a grave, though tearless mien ;
Her rose cheek and bright brow shaden
   By rich locks as e'er were seen.

In her tiny hand enfolded
   Was a bunch of fragrant flowers :
Such a form in beauty moulded
   Graces seldom earthly bowers.

Ever and anon she scatter'd
   Blossoms on that lowly mound,
Though the autumn raindrops patter'd
   And the dead leaves fell around.

Truly 'twas a scene of beauty—
    Calm and still the shadows lay—
There beside Love's grave sat Duty
    Mournful homage still to pay.

From the antique porch the robin
    Sang a sweet melodious song;
In a field adjacent, Dobbin
    Drew the noiseless plough along.

By the grave the little maiden
    Answ'ring questions ask'd by me,
With her brow by bright curls shaden,
    Told her own sad history.

THE LITTLE MAID'S STORY.

" It is my own dear mother sleeps
    Beneath the dark yew's shade,
At home no father sits and weeps
    The havoc Death has made.

" He left us in the early spring
    Across the seas to roam,
And even summer fail'd to bring
    The dear one to our home.

" With anxious eye my mother
    For many a sad day sate,
Seeking her grief to smother
    Though left so desolate.

" Through the long night she listen'd,
    But father never came ;
At last her tear-drops glisten'd
    At mention of his name.

" I sought in vain to soothe her,
    Indeed I did my best ;
And our good pastor told her
    To look to God for rest.

" I saw her colour flying
    I did, sir, day by day ;
But knew not she was dying
    Or like to pass away.

" Until one eve she call'd me
    To sit down by her side,
And gaz'd at me so wistfully
    That somehow, sir, I cried.

" For the knowledge burst upon me,
    That she was call'd away ;
And sobbing, sobbing piteously
    I begg'd of her to stay.

" But with a look of gentleness,
    Just like the angel wears,
That's cloth'd in robes of holiness,
    Close by the altar stairs—

" You know the picture sir," she said,
    " It was my mother's pet,
And when I look at it, though dead,
    I seem to see her yet !

" She drew me nearer to her side,
    And kissing all my face,
Said, ' Little one, you're sorely tried,
    But God will give you grace.

" ' He wills it I should leave you, love,
    And leave you lonely too,
But from my home of rest above,
    I shall look down on you.

" ' So mind that you are good, and do
    Your very best whilst here—
Love God, and love your neighbour too,
    And then you need not fear.

" ' And if your father should come home
    From o'er the stormy sea,
Tell him, my darling one, to come
    And share my Heav'n with me!'

Then, sir, she mov'd her lips in pray'r,
    And whilst I sobb'd and cried,
Death's arrow speeded through the air,
    And, blessing God, she died.

" I have done all my very best
    To follow in her track,
For though she lieth there 'at rest,
    Her words, they oft come back !

" And when my father dear returns
    From o'er the distant sea,
If love within his heart still burns
    He'll visit her with me.

" I know he will—and therefore I
    Am often, often here—
And when God calls me I shall lie
    Close by my mother dear."

She ceas'd ; and with a lavish hand
    Scatter'd her wealth of flow'rs—
The ev'ning shades crept up the land
    As noiseless as the hours.

The robin from the antique porch
    Warbled his farewell lay ;
And the broad shadow of the church
    Across the greensward lay.

Truly it was a quiet scene—
   The grave, and that maiden fair,
With her starry eyes where tears had been,
   And her locks of golden hair.

And on her brow and on her cheek
   Not a tint of earth to dim
The light of a spirit pure and meek
   That shone from the soul within!

     *   *   *

Oh! often I've dreamt in the round of life
   Of that peaceful churchyard scene;
And that little maid 'midst all its strife
   My angel guide hath been.

When clouds were dark, I've sought the Ark
   That to her bright faith seem'd near,
And when all alone have heard her tone
   Whisper, "You need not fear!"

I know not if her father came
   From o'er the distant sea;
But I feel that she watches there the same
   Beneath the dark yew tree.

And that her life in the fullest sense
   Responds to the mother's pray'r —
That they'll meet again when she goes from hence
   The same bright home to share!

"IT IS BUT FOR A TIME."

It is but for a time—bear up,
   Thou sad and drooping soul;
Drink to the dregs life's bitter cup,
   Stand fast in self-control.

Dost grieve the lov'd are cold and chang'd?
    Dost weep with bitter tears
Affection's vows that unestrang'd
    Were thine for long bright years?

The Summer of thy youth is gone,
    The Autumn coming now,
And Winter soon his snowy zone
    Will bind upon thy brow.

But after Winter comes the Spring!
   . Glad form to bless the earth!
So from the grave of Hope may spring
    Flow'rs of a brighter birth.

Scatter all sadness to the blast,
    Hold with a tighten'd hand
The red Cross, till the storm be past—
    Firmer in faith thou'lt stand.

And for the cares that vex thee here,
    A sure reward be giv'n.
Poor exile in an alien sphere,
    Thine, a glad home in Heav'n!

FAREWELL.

FAREWELL, farewell, my precious one,
    The wide sea parts us now,
Yet not so much the foaming waves,
    That dash against thy prow,
As the cold stormy wind of change
    That sweeps across thy brow.

A few short hours, a fresh fair wind,
    And thou wilt far away
Banish all kindly memory
    Of her who writes this lay ;
Of her who sorrowful and lone
    Dwells on the parting day.

The northern billows soon will rock
    Thee to thy nightly sleep ;
But will they bring as calm a rest,
    As holy and as deep,
As erst in bygone years was thine,
    Ere Faith had learn'd to weep ?

Ere 'twixt our souls the yawning gulf
    Of stormy conflict pass'd,
Ere other hearts had claim'd a love
    To which I held so fast ;
And which was all in all to me,
    Oh, God ! though lost at last !

Thou hast no clinging memories
    Of the dear vanish'd day,
When I was in thy cherish'd sight
    What thou'rt to me alway.
No, no ! the cold hard world has prest
    Faith's embers to decay !

I see thee still stand by my side,
    I feel thy hand in mine,
And watch Affection's holy light
    Beam from those eyes of thine ;
Whilst the pale daybreak struggles forth,
    And stars forget to shine.

I've nothing but that memory now
  To cheer my coming days ;
The Star of Hope burnt faint a while,
  And then withdrew her rays.
The mists of dark despair obscure
  Too oft my tearful gaze!

The world has spread its lures for thee,
  And flow'ry paths and sweet,
Where thorns lie hidden 'neath the turf
  Attract thy careless feet.
I would give all my sun of life
  To save thee from deceit!

Oh! that each true and honest heart
  Some day may seem most dear!
Oh! that above the grave of love
  Thou may'st but shed one tear,
To wash out all the changeful past,
  And make God's Heav'n more near!

Hadst thou remain'd what once thou wert,
  Only in love for me,
Then had I bless'd each other change
  And pray'd my God for thee :
Not in deep anguish e'en as now,
  But in serenity!

One little hope—one tiny one—
  Sweetens Life's bitter cup,
And bids me drain the poison'd bowl
  Of Disappointment up ;
'Tis that a judgment-day must come,
  Accounts be rendered up!

Then do I know that upright love,
  Like mine, will meet its due ;
Then do I feel all will be right
  Once more 'twixt me and you :
And the plain truth in flaming words
  Appear before the view !

This life at best is but a path
  Unto the better land ;
A rugged one to some it seems,
  Whilst others calmly stand,
Waiting for the eternal shore
  Like brothers, hand in hand.

I could have waited thus with thee,
  Have watch'd the ev'ning fall,
Rejoicing that the coming night
  Would cast its shades o'er all ;
Hoping we two at least stood firm,
  Waiting our final call.

But now another hand holds thine
  In a too fast embrace ;
Another heart takes all thy love
  And drives me from my place.
Oh ! bitter, bitter memory,
  That nothing can efface !

Hast thou not faith for both ? or shall
  The friend of years depart
Upon her lonely walk in life
  With sad and wither'd heart ?
Feeling that one she lov'd too well
  Play'd an unworthy part !

Yet not so—what am I to thee?
  And what are Love and Faith?
But spectres beck'ning from the arms
  Of some deluding wraith!
Who seeks to lure the passers by
  To change, deceit, and death!

Oh, God! that we had never met,
  Or had not lov'd so well;
Then were we both on even terms
  In bidding our farewell!
Then were the pangs unknown to me
  Which words can never tell!

Adieu, adieu, my precious one,
  Mine ever—though we part—
Full many a tearful thought of mine
  Will follow where thou art;
And be 't in weal, or be 't in woe,
  Thy name live in my heart!

DREAM THOUGHTS.

FROM "EVA" AND OTHER POEMS.

DIMLY doth each twinkling star
  Peep from the wintry sky;
Howls the chill north wind from afar,
  And tempest clouds skim by.
Wearily, yes wearily, I think of moments that are
    gone,
And thy spirit-heart responds to mine with clear and
    thrilling tone!

Time was when we together
  Fought 'gainst the ills of life;
But now the clouds that gather
  Portend for thee no strife.

I wrap myself in silent dreams, and mirror back the
    past,
Whilst thou, immortal, shar'st the light o'er happy
    spirits cast !

Calmly seems thy pale grey eye
    To watch me from its home,
With the same mournful look that I
    Have seen in hours long flown.
What would I give to be with thee beyond life's pain
    and ill,
Or that thy holy sympathy fill'd all my spirit still.

Thickly the snow-flakes falling
    Cover the earth with white,
And goblin arms appalling
    Seem stretching on the night.
The frozen ground, encased in ice, crispeth beneath my
    tread,
And the dead leaves rustle drearily above thy narrow bed.

Would I were there with thee, love,
    Beneath the chilly sod,
The mystery of death unwove,
    To live again with God.
But no ! thro' earth's dim wilderness my weary feet
    must stray,
These darken'd eyes still pining for the light that's
    pass'd away !

Borne on the wings of thought
    To thy far land I soar ;
Many a holy spell, dream wrought,
    Circling my spirit o'er ;
And the cloud-cappëd earth seems then to me like a
    little speck that lies
'Neath the fiery sun when it sinks to rest in the purple
    ev'ning skies !

And I marvel if thy love
  Clings to my spirit still,
If in the spheres of light above
  One human thought may thrill ;
Or if cold and passionless thou art, like a river's icy
    bound,
That no more may pour its waters forth in a free glad
    stream around.

Alas ! still veil'd in mystery,
  The future as the past !
Voiceless my soul soars up to thee,
  Oh ! shall we meet at last ?
Would that an answ'ring sound might swell thro' the
    deep midnight sky,
Or the chill night-wind murmur forth one faint affirming
    cry !

But silent all.   Tired Nature,
  Folded in wintry veil,
Ice-bound in every feature,
  Glares round with aspect pale.
And the cruel universe, with scorn, seems mocking at
    my woe,
Oh ! that afar, to Joy's dream-land, my clouded soul
    might go !

Then never more Doubt's fever
  Should burn in every vein,
Nor Hope, the base deceiver,
  Make me her sport again.
Amidst the amaranthine bow'rs of perfect bliss I'd
    roam,
And greet thee, my belovëd one, in thy far deathless
    home !

THE DOWNHILL OF LIFE.

I HAVE gain'd the mountain top, and now
   With a steady gaze look down,
Where the waters of life beneath me flow
In a winding stream, through a course I know,
   'Midst forests that grimly frown.

On their bosom reflected I trace the past,
   Its dangers, its terrors, and all
The once cherish'd delights which we held so fast,
Until o'er their glories a dark cloud past,
   Like a thick funereal pall.

I can mark the haunts where in early hours
   My childish footsteps stray'd,
And can see the sunshine gild the bowers
Which to our young sight were so gay with flowers,
   Which we never dreamt could fade.

The voices once lov'd—they are thrilling yet,
   E'en yet, through my dizzy brain;
Their words, alas! I can never forget,
For through the pale mists of a life's regret
   They come to my heart again!

Where are the forms that across my dreams
   Through so many an hour have pass'd?
Where are the gay and the golden gleams
Of the early morning's rich sunbeams?
   Alas! into night they 've pass'd!

E'en so have those forms from my pathway gone,
   E'en so has their glory shaded!
And the light of the heart that within them shone,
Burnt out like a fire, but to leave more lone,
   The path whence their love has faded.

K

Not one of the many delights of youth
    Are left to my spirit now,
There are long-lost visions of love and truth,
There are sick'ning thoughts of the cold world's ruth,
    That o'er me like dark waves flow.

But I feel that the paths I once have trod
    I must never walk again,
For I stand alone on the earth's damp sod,
And my thoughts and hopes must arise to God,
    Whom we never serve in vain !

From the mountain heights which my soul hath climb'd,
    I feel I must now descend,
No longings—no yearnings of heart or mind,
But a meek endurance —a faith resign'd,
    And a thought of the coming end !

These with the strength and the earnest will
    To do all the good I can,
To solace the suff'ring, and seek to still
All thoughts of evil and pain that fill
    The breasts of my fellow-man ;

Must now be life's portion—must lead me on
    Through the latter days, whose light
When this dim world's mists are past and gone,
And up from the darkness springs the moon,
    Will be purely—calmly bright.

But leading to brighter and better—where
    The sun in its fullest glory
Shall shine on the hearts of all whose pray'r
Through the sin and sorrow—the pain and care,
    Which saddens our human story,

Has been to conquer, to win at last,
    That pure and perfect being,
Which, when the snares of this life are past,
And the grain sprung up which was sown broadcast,
    Shall be ours, THOU Great All-Seeing !

JOHN HARRIS.

SINCE the first appearance of the much-admired contributions of this esteemed writer to the pages of the " Poetical Souvenir," we beg to acknowledge the receipt of a little volume, from which we have derived great pleasure, entitled " Wandering Cries," (London : Partridge and Co.) It would be expressive of high praise to say, that the following poems from the same pen are fair specimens of the contents of this little book, but that would scarcely be doing it justice. It consists of a beautiful series of short poems, which the mere rhymester could scarcely appreciate, but which a true poet would welcome with surprise and delight. We have not met with a volume during the season to which we have referred with greater satisfaction. It is full of rich poetic thoughts elegantly expressed, with a musical rhythm suggestive of the author's unmistakable genius. It deserves to be well known and largely circulated. The author desires us to acknowledge the permission of Mr. Charles Dickens to republish the beautiful lines entitled " The Future," from " All the Year Round."

LITTLE MAY.

I hope you're not forgetting,
   Little May;
Though now so far above
The reach of earthly love,
The happiness God sent us in the summers pass'd
  away,
When we wandered hand in hand
About the pleasant land,
With the sunlight in our hearts, and all was bright
  and gay,
   Little May !

But now I'm weeping, weeping,
                Little May ;
As I wander all apart,
With a shadow in my heart,
For I want your smile again to shine and make it
        day :
A pretty bud were you,
That by the river grew,
And the water came to love you, and floated you
        away,
                Little May !

My soul will follow after
                Little May ;
For I'm a flower too,
Though not so bright as you,
And I'm floating down the river that has carried
        you away ;
And on a happy shore,
We shall bloom for evermore,
In the sunny summer-weather of a never-dying day,
                Little May !

THE EMPTY HEART.

On the rocky shore,
    All alone it lies,
" Come to me, bright shapes,
    Come to me," it cries.

" Come to me," it longs,
    But the waves are tost
Roughly on the shore,
    And the cry is lost.

"Come to me," it weeps,
"All things good and high,
All hearts that can love,
Come, or I shall die."

Peace! oh, troubled heart,
God will ease thy pain;
Longing for the true
Cannot be in vain.

All the faces fair
Thou dost seem to see
Are not of the earth,
Yet they wait for thee.

Kingcups needing rain,
Drooping faint and dull,
Upward look, and wait
Till God makes them full.

So, with child-like trust,
Look up, empty heart;
God will come to thee,
Helpless as thou art.

Dried are all the tears,
Still'd the longings wild,
When the mother comes
To the crying child.

THE FUTURE.

THE drop that falls unnoted in the stream,
Prattling in childhood on its native hill;
The stream that must leave home and travel far
Over rough ways, with torn feet and no rest,
Changing its voice, and then, in calmer flow,

Sobered by dreams of the eternal sea,
Pass with wide water, trembling in its depths,
To the great ocean, like a soul to Heaven,
And bear the drop to rest, and roam no more.

For me, a life that only late set out,
In weakness, as a swallow from the nest,
On its long journey to the land unknown,
That, gaining strength, must pass through stony ways,
Be lashed of storms, and ofttimes, in thick gloom,
Lose sight of what it prized, yet with the hope
That all its blighted loves and treasures lost
Are taken of the wind, like wingëd seeds,
And sown by angels in the better land,
Where this tired life shall rest, and find them grown.

The beam that, distant yet, but on its way
Intent, passed systems, over comet-tracks,
Comes like a pilgrim with an offering,
And through the pure space to the misty world
Brings the faint greeting of a star unknown.

For me, the light feet, not yet heard on earth,
That move toward me from the better land,
And, though unheeded, shall complete their work,
And, like the morning sunburst breaking night,
When my heart faints, and all my life is dark,
Step from the cloud, bearing the gift of Heaven,
Sweet face and tender hands to comfort me.

The poet that shall come in the world's need
And lead men to the light, and teach them truth,
And win them by the wonder of his words,
Till true be known for true, and false for false,
And build the many-coloured bow of thought
In sight above their heads, and, in the end,
From his gold cup shall so enrich the world
That men shall lavish blessings on his grave.

For me the angel that shall take my hand,
When winds are ceasing, and my work is done,
And, like a king leading a beggar child,
Shall open death and lead me through the veil,
And gently guide me, dazzled with the light,
Till my hand rests on all that I have lost.

INVISIBLE FLOWERS.

OFTEN, through things which we might dare to scorn,
  Some movement of a leaf, or breath of wind,
Some sudden trifle, an idea is born
  Which had not its beginning in the mind;
Through some bright cloud or tree of deepening green,
  A new thought bursts to being, wondrous fair,
Blooming in Nature as a flower unseen,
  For they who pass know not that it is there.

Such flower will oft to sudden beauty spring,
  Seen for a moment of the passer-by
Who stores not in his heart the fragile thing,
  And, thus uncared for, it will quickly die;
But clearer grows its form to Poet's view,
  Who for such beauty eagerly doth long,
And, willing that the world should love it too,
  Takes it with care and plants it in his song.

There rooted, through all seasons doth it shine
  Unvarying, and in brightest hues arrayed,
To true sight visible, and will not pine,
  But blooms as heavenly flower which cannot fade;
And, when loss grieves us, and we feel the smart,
  Sweet comfort brightens through its beauty rare,
And its pure odour steals into the heart
  Until our spirits breathe a finer air.

THE SINGING BIRD.

OH, child of fancy, fairer than the morn,
    For whom my life strives like a baffled wave,
Oh, bright and good, but who art yet unborn,
    And in the far-off years shalt cross my grave,
Draw near and listen, with compassion sweet,
    For in this verse, as in a summer tree,
With notes that soar through time toward thy feet,
    A tiny bird lies hid, and sings for thee.

For thee, for thee! but wilt thou hear the song,
    Learnt in the woods and simple though it be,
And shall it into silence fade ere long,
    Or may kind echoes waft it on to thee?
Ah! beautiful, forgive the foolish bird
    Whose fluttering heart is even now distress'd,
And trembling lest the notes fall back unheard,
    And buried lie, with all the broken nest.

TOO LATE.

"OH! violet of mine, conceal'd from view,
    Let me once find the nook where thou dost lie,
Hide not, for I am as a drop of dew
    That would but sink into thy breast and die!
The timid leaves shall open without fear,
    For I will plant thee in a garden fine,
Where streams and bright-wing'd birds shall wander
        near,
    To make sweet music round thee, love of mine!"

Too late the cry!—not all for thee, weak heart,
    The flower thou dreamest of was here display'd!
Nor could it linger, having done its part;
    Should not God have it ere its beauty fade?

Yet hast thou power, if thou wilt wisely heed,
  To reproduce the hues thou canst not see,
For the thought thus left in thee is a seed,
  And something like the flower may grow in thee!

IN VAIN.

To the same well-known tune the waters flow,
  While trembles my weak heart, admitting fears
With foolish memories of long ago,
  Of yearnings, now decayed, then built with tears;
And, looking back, and wanting strength, I say,
  " Time brings rich hours and lays them in my hand,
But, as pearls, I have let them slip away,
  And must I ever lose them on the sand?"

Ah! let them not be vain, not all in vain,
  The happy days that will return no more,
The faces that I shall not see again,
  The youthful dreaming on the summer shore;
But give me as a little star to shine,
  And, though unknown, to touch with light some
    hours
In lives of better, purer souls than mine,
  As unseen dewdrops minister to flowers.

MY MISTRESS.

My love, so little worth, I give to her,
Who, dwelling far above us in the cloud,
Is fair beyond the beauty of the world,
And Queen for ever, if we heed or not.

Her highest throne is in the heart of God,
And angels, at a distance moving round,
Sing in the glory which we cannot see;
Her sceptre is all-pure and beautiful,
More like a flower than anything on Earth,
Her face is holy, and her name is TRUTH.

Far off, and in the mist, but known to me,
She shines, and draws me, and I follow her,
And move toward her feebly through the gloom,
And work for her, and for her good would die.

My life is hers, and, should I gain a crown,
Not for myself I win it, but for her,
And humbly to her feet shall bring the prize,
And all the beauties gathered in the world
I will weave in a garland to crown her,
And she shall rule, and men shall know her fair.

Oh! be my work ever so weak and small,
To her I shall go begging, " Take it, Queen,
Here is the little bloom of all I did,
And here the blind life-struggle melts in rest;"
Then will she drive me back :—" Hence ! untrue life !"
Or tremble over me, with pitying wings,
And plant the snow-white flower in my heart.

LOSSES.

IN a Poet's heart
  Seeds of thought were sown
Which would bless the Earth,
  Could he make them known.

But the truth within,
  He could not rehearse,
Couldn't make a flower
  Of the cumbrous verse.

So through life he pin'd
  For the gift denied,
Whisper'd, but unheard,
  Strove, and wept, and died.

Then the silent soul
  On its mission went,
For not to the world
  Was the message sent.

The nest-bird that dies
  Ere fledged are its wings,
Has the tune within,
  Though it never sings.

In the tiny seed
  Lay the flower-thought,
Which in feeble leaves
  For expression sought.

But the North wind blew
  With a sudden blight,
Ere the hidden hues
  Could break into sight.

Yet is nothing lost,
  Though the voice is weak,
For God must be heard,
  When He wills to speak ;

And the flowers of truth
  In the dust may fall,
But shall bloom again,
  For God keeps them all.

A CHILD-WISH.

I SIT upon the meadow-grass,
    With flowers blooming round,
Meek daisies, clover, buttercups,
    All common on the ground;
Their beauty bears the stamp of Heaven,
    And fills me with delight,
For thus God's blessing on the Earth
    Comes struggling into sight.

Oh! I would be a flower too,
    In brightest hues array'd,
With breath that should as incense rise,
    Until my time to fade;
Then I would fearlessly bend down,
    And, kissing the pure sod,
Would rest my leaves on such sweet earth,
    And give my soul to God.

Some new charm I would leave behind
    That should not quickly pass,
Like the sweet odour of the hay,
    Which clings not to the grass;
And, ere my memory on Earth
    Could fade from friendly view,
God would have made me grow in Heaven,
    And marked my leaves anew.

BROTHERS ALL.

SHALL our lives, with power to soar,
    Still in envious discord fall,
Striving which can greater be,
    Who by birth are brothers all;

While we work, not side by side,
Our best Heaven is lost through pride,
Lost the strength we might impart
    Were we bound in love together,
    Breasting so the stormy weather,
Hand in hand and heart in heart!

For we are but children here,
    Needing oft the chastening rod,
And in this school are maintained
    Through the charity of God;
If we listen when He pleads,
If we follow where He leads,
And do not too widely roam,
    When the years have pass'd away,
    To our endless holiday
Our Great Friend will take us home.

THE LITTLE STREAM.

By Heaven on a loving mission sent,
    Into the world she came—a simple child;
But flowers unbidden sprang up where'er she went,
    And in her features light and comfort smiled.
Her life flowed by us like a little stream
    That sings, and in its breast reflects the sky;
Until we found, on waking from a dream,
    The music silenced and the channel dry.

Sometimes I seem to hear the step I know
    Come, with sweet voice or laughter, down the hill,
As one, who knows where waters used to flow,
    May stand and think he hears them prattling still;
And her face, when I dream of happier hours,
    Shines from the gloom, repeating some bright look,
In spots she loved, as shades of water-flowers
    May haunt the margins of that dried-up brook.

The hand whose soft touch lingers warm on mine,
  The smile that often rippled on her face,
The eyes that lately used on us to shine,
  Have passed from earth to light another place ;
Her voice is now the music of a dream ;
  We wake to silence, and are all unblest,
For the bright waters of this little stream
  Have gained the sea before their time, and rest.

AN OLD HAUNT.

THE path goes winding to the beach below,
  Held sacred to the days that come no more—
Shell-gemmed, and rich as any spot I know
  In sea-pinked rocks and wonders of the shore ;
But now that years with change have hurried by,
  And the same light feet never linger there,
Ought not its beauties one by one to die,
  Like flowers orphaned of a tender care ?

Nay ! there let Nature show her fairest face,
  And smile, when our small lives are swept away,
For we would not throw shade on that bright place,
  Nor, with poor memories, mote the eye of day ;
Let the same song swell from the untaught sea,
  And, to the rocks, as lovely flowers cling,
For 'mid such beauteous scenes, what more are we
  Than withered leaves which clothed a buried spring ?

SWEET FACES.

CHILD-FACES round us beaming,
  How wonderful they are !
So pale and common-seeming,
  Yet each a perfect star ;

In every crowded city
　These new conceits have birth,
And thoughts of God in pity
　Are thus express'd on Earth.

When Katie's face I'm viewing,
　If she's at work or play,
Whatever she is doing,
　She leads my mind away
To where bright birds are winging
　Swift flight from tree to tree,
And songs to her are singing,
　Or so it seems to me.

There's Rose, a little lady,
　Now nearly ten years old,
So quaint and so old-maidy,
　So shy and yet so bold;
In all she says so clever,
　In all she does so kind,
And sunlight shines for ever
　Her gravest looks behind.

There's Annie, always smiling,
　I think she cannot frown,
That smile is so beguiling,
　Oh! could I write it down!
Oh! could I to these pages
　The perfect charm impart,
To bind through all the ages
　The deathless human heart!

If one sweet face has vanished
　That seemed to us Divine,
'Tis only we are banished,
　Yet are not left to pine;

For freely in all places,
    As flowers from the sod,
Spring up these childish faces,
    So bountiful is God!

———◦◦———

THE CHARMÈD RING.

FORGETFUL of the daylight almost fled,
    A child sits on the richly-painted grou nd,
With daisy-crown white-glimmering on her head,
    And all her bliss in treasures blooming round;
Calm flows her life, content with its own powers,
    And troubles, when they gloom so sweet a face,
Flit as bird-shadows over meadow flowers:
    At length Sleep finds her there, and charms the
        place.

A glow surpassing light of stars or moon
    Deepens about her while, from bluebells near,
Bright shapes surprise her, gliding forth, and soon,
    As she were Queen, move round her without fear;
" From this sweet dream," she prays, " I would not
        wake,"
    And rapt beholds them link'd as flowers in chain,
Heedless that, flying by, they round her make
    The charmèd ring that none can pass again.

Silent she lies, by morn exposed to view,
    The phantom-memory of a lost delight,
The daisies round her forehead blind with dew,
    The smile reflecting something out of sight;
Ah! it was Love that on her cast a beam,
    As helpless 'mid the flowers of life she lay,
And what appeared but fairies in her dream
    Were angels sent to bear the soul away.

CLOUD-SPRITES.

OF Fairies and House-sprites erewhile I told you,
  The stories sung to me by some wild bird,
Of what bright eyes from tiny flowers behold you,
  But of Cloud-sprites I think you never heard.

Yet are they born with sunlight in the morning,
  For one day's life of bright and happy flow,
And when white clouds are all the sky adorning,
  Unseen by us, they climb their hills of snow.

These airy shapes with which our world is haunted
  Are hidden in the grosser light of day,
Lest by their beauty we should be enchanted,
  And, loving, seek to follow them away.

Sometimes to earth, with early sunbeam-showers,
  They fly, and roam the blooming fields about,
And with delight hang over common flowers,
  And kiss the fairy-faces peeping out.

When day is done, with pity vast and tender,
  They look out on us from the western sky,
And what we blindly call the sunset-splendour
  Shines where they meet to pass away or die.

Thus they depart, and then the moon grows stately,
  And here and there shines out a feeble spark,
And in the west, where glory blossom'd lately,
  Like silence after music comes the dark.

And then it seems,—but this is fancy only—
  .That star-tears glittering on the face of night,
And the earth clothed in shadow, sad and lonely,
  Show Nature's grief for their too-rapid flight.

Either they fly to where new suns are beaming,
  Or seek long rest on Heaven's starry floor,
As, in the milk-way, eyes grown wild with dreaming
  May find their forms sleep-bound for evermore.

L

WIND-SPRITES.

COME round me this wild night, oh, children dear,
    And as we sit thus quiet and alone,
Something I'll tell you while the storm we hear :
    Hark! how it roars, then dies into a moan!

You never knew whence came that sullen roar,
    Nor that low wailing melancholy cry,
But when you hear it now, for evermore,
    You'll say, " There are the Wind-sprites passing by."

They are the evil Fairies, and they dwell
    In those rank weeds that grow far out at sea ;
And thence inland they roam o'er hill and dell,
    While all good spirits from their presence flee.

They ride the storm-rack, making Heaven their own,
    So that Cloud-sprites at eve will not appear ;
They look through windows, to our sight unknown,
    But House-sprites see, and hide in trembling fear.

With shrieks untuneful, through the Summer-bowers
    They rush, good fairies filling with affright,
And breathe upon and touch the helpless flowers,
    And roughly shake, and sometimes break them quite.

So through the storm they show their wicked hate,
    But, wearied in the end, some peace would win,
And turn to sea-wastes where the great weeds wait
    With dark arms to embrace and take them in.

To those strange isles unknown to human eye
    Homeward they wander when the tempest fails,
And often see the white-winged ships go by,
    And long to come to them and tear the sails.

Or else their shadowy army flies in rout, .
    Driven and made the sport of some strong wind,
And, falling on their damp beds wearied out,
    Would sleep, but perfect rest they never find.

There is no rest but for the good, my dears,
   So love each other, and be pure and true,
And guard, with jealous care, for brighter spheres
   The sprites that look your blooming faces through.

———◦∘◦———

SUNDAY-SCHOOL SONG.

For happiness on earth
   We ever seek in vain,
For we fail in loving,
   And we suffer pain;
But there they feed on love,
   The bread of Heaven is love;
Therefore we shall happy be
   When we meet above!

There we shall work for love
   In all we have to do;
Angels bright will love us,
   And God will love us too;
'Twill be love, love, love,
   There's nothing there but love,
Therefore we shall happy be
   When we meet above!

The love we gather here,
   Half opened, fades away;
Either friends forget us
   Or they must not stay;
But there it's deathless love!
   It's everlasting love!
Therefore we shall happy be
   When we meet above!

———◦∘◦———

BLESSING.

Oh! you for whom I link this chain of words,
  Friends in the world who cheer me every day,
You that light up the town, and you, sweet birds
  Whose nest is by the river, miles away;
And you, far off, whom mighty seas divide,
  Dwelling on strange shores, ever out of call;
My pearls that o'er the earth are scattered wide,
  Through the dim space I cry, "God bless you all!"

Fair child that, nurtured on the ocean-shore,
  Hast been sea-taught through all a happy youth,
May love-stars light thy life for evermore,
  And thou, sweet bud, not ope to less than truth:
God keep thee while the hours of silence creep,
  And let no unkind dream come near to thee,
Who, resting out of sight, art deaf in sleep
  To this cry and the moaning of the sea.

Such weak-winged blessings wander in the air,
  Like that ark-dove, whose feet could find no rest,
And cannot carry comfort anywhere,
  But die, unless God guide them to the nest;
Then have they power to cheer the midnight gloom
  As if with bird-songs, and, though vain it seems,
Sleepers within, when morning lights the room,
  Wake comforted by music heard in dreams.

SYDNEY HODGES.

TOGETHER with the accompanying original poems we acknowledge the receipt of a volume, entitled "The Battle of Hastings, and other Poems" (Simpkin, Marshall, and Co.), by the above-named writer, and although the volume was printed some years ago, it is of too much poetical value to be soon forgotten. We extract the beautiful poems entitled, "Angels' Visits" and "Daisy Bell." These, however, are not altogether fair specimens of the author's varied style; and we feel assured, should our readers procure the volume, they will not blame us for our word of commendation. The poems are full of quiet, unaffected pathos, the emanations evidently of a mind influenced not only by the beautiful and true in nature, but with a desire to propagate the highest and purest aspirations. The volume is most creditable, and well deserves the warm encouragement and thanks which its author has received from the great poet of America, Professor Longfellow. We thank Mr. Hodges for his original compositions, and trust, in future volumes, he will sustain his well-merited reputation.

OLD AND NEW.

THE sky is dark, the night-winds blow,
The new year cometh not with snow,
But with a mournful wailing low ;

And moisture on the soddened earth—
A sorry night—a sorry birth—
And in my heart no tone of mirth.

The old old year is dying fast—
I look into the mournful past,
And feel with sorrow overcast.

So little said, so little done
Since the dying year was first begun,
And I had hope like every one.

Afar, the household fires are bright—
And many a jest goes round to-night
In halls with shining holly dight.

I sit alone and watch the year
Pass sadly on his sable bier—
I feel an awful Presence near;

That with the wailing of the seas,
Comes up upon the midnight breeze,
And stands among the shivering trees,

Enfolding, with a gesture dread,
The pall around the old year dead,
And holds the future months outspread;

With space for pure resolves again,
With more of joy—with less of pain,
With more of Christ—with less of Cain.

ON THE SEA.

OVER the side of the vessel,
  Bearing me on to my home,
Silently leaning I listen
  To the low tongues in the foam.
Spirit-like voices more tender
  Than the soft rain through the trees,
Dying in measureless splendour,
  Over the measureless seas.

Up from the blue depths of ocean,
　Roused by the beat of the wheel,
Theirs is the music of motion,
　Theirs is the rapture I feel.
Lifting their white arms in greeting,
　Where the waves follow and fall;
Whisp'ring to me of a meeting
　Sweeter, ah! sweeter than all.

Through the long night I have hearkened
　To the loud roar of the train,
Bearing me, when the eve darkened,
　Back to the ocean again.
There, when Day's moments were numbered,
　Stars that had soared beyond sight
Dropped to the ocean and slumbered
　On the still waves through the night.

Over the side of the vessel,
　Bearing me on to my home,
Languidly leaning I listen
　To the low song of the foam.
Singing, oh! singing not only
　Songs of the rocks and the sand,
But of the forest glades lonely
　Far in the leaf-laden land.

Songs they have learnt of the river
　Flowing from moorlands afar,
Flowing for ever and ever
　Down to the wave-fringëd bar:
Flowing for ever and ever,
　Flowing by forest and plain,
Backward returning, oh never,
　To the bleak moorland again.

Only when spring tides are burning
   Over the sun-glowing sand,
Landward old Ocean returning
   Takes the lost stream in his hand.
Then for a moment the river
   Sees the far hills of its home,
Ere it departeth for ever
   Over the desolate foam.

Sad! that it cannot revisit
   The rapid, the moss, or the fern.
Pleasure or destiny is it
   That seems to forbid its return?
Destiny is it, or pleasure,
   That bears us along like the stream,
Lulled by a magical measure,
   Lulled in a beautiful dream?

SONNET.

TO JOHN HARRIS.

Thou tread'st a world apart.   Thy ears are hushed
To the loud bickerings of the bitter world;
And like a stately ship, with canvas furled,
Moveless upon the bay—so sits thy soul
Upon the tide which we call human life.
The sinews of thy growing mind have crushed
The fiends that baffle others in the strife,
Ill-guided passions, and the sins that roll
With avalanche power down-crushing the pure buds
Of Virtue.   Like the conquerer Cortes thou
On Orizaba's slope, with silver floods
And golden plains far stretched beneath, for now
The plains of life, thought-sown, beneath thee shine;
And Cortes-like thou criest, " These are mine."

ANGELS' VISITS.

Angels !
Ye visit us sometimes,
   When the mild morn doth glow ;
And the soft sabbath chimes
   Swell through the vale below.
When 'mid the golden furze,
On the green upland slope we calmly lie,
Where the bright, dewy cowslip scarcely stirs,
   As the slow breeze goes by.
When from the meadows fair,
   Where star-eyed daisies nod,
The lone heart's quiet prayer
   Goes calmly up to God,
The peace of spirits blest
Comes to the inward breast ;
   Telling of angels near,
      Angels' visits.

Angels !
Ye visit us in sleep :
   Your footsteps round us tread,
Light as the night hours creep,
   Around the silent bed.
After long weeks of pain,
When from the first sweet sleep we wake once more,
And feel the glow of coming health again,
   In limbs so faint before,
Thoughts of the world and sin,
   Long past, all seem to cease ;
And purer ones creep in,
   And all the soul is peace.
The calm of spirits blest
Comes to the inward breast ;
   Telling of angels near,
      Angels' visits.

Angels !
We feel your presence near,
    When golden stars awaken ;
And through the twilight clear,
    Soft dews from heaven are shaken.
When the lulled ocean lies,
Calm as on that fair morn that saw its birth ;
And the soul soars beyond the distant skies,
    That darken o'er the earth.
When not a lingering breath
    Fans the soft cheek of Heaven ;
And stillness deep as death
    To the wrapt world is given.
The peace of spirits blest
Then stirs the inward breast ;
    Telling of angels near,
        Angels' visits.

Angels !
Ye visit us in love,
    When in the night of care,
To the great God above,
    We pour our contrite prayer.
When with a brother's heart,
We strive to soothe the pangs of want and sickness ;
And of our wealth or scantness spare a part,
    In unpretending meekness.
When, in the grief of sin,
    We raise to Heaven our fears ;
And cleanse the soul within
    With penitential tears.
The peace of spirits blest
Then comes to soothe the breast ;
    Telling of angels near,
        Angels' visits.

DAISY-BELL.

DAISY-BELL, Daisy-bell,
I know my heart would love you well :
For like soft music, sweetly clear,
Your name is chiming in my ear.
So softly sweet the name you bear,
    You must be some rare star of earth,
Far shining with a light so fair,
    That all have loved you from your birth.
Though I have never been so blest,
    As on those living charms to dwell,
You're fondly imaged in my breast,
    Daisy-bell, sweet Daisy-bell.

Daisy-bell, Daisy-bell,
Where soft the waves at midnight fell,
I roamed in silent ecstasy,
With your sweet sister by the sea.
The melancholy moonlight lay
    In silver lines along the deep ;
And over all the wide, wild bay,
    A tone of sadness seemed to creep.
At that mild, melancholy hour,
    She spoke, as I remember well,
A name that had a magic power,
    And that sweet name was Daisy-bell.

Daisy-bell, Daisy-bell,
I cannot, oh ! I cannot tell
The visions sweet that seemed to rise,
And float before my charmëd eyes.
The words, like magic, seemed to bring
    All fairy dreams and fancies light ;
The breath and beauty of the spring
    Came back with all its green delight.

I saw your eyes, whose hue outshines
   The hyacinth within the dell;
Your hair that o'er your forehead twines,
   In golden bands, sweet Daisy-bell.

   Daisy-bell, Daisy-bell,
The flower whose name you wear so well,
Is not more pure, and fresh, and bright,
Than your warm soul of love and light.
Your voice is softer than the sound
   Of summer breezes through the leaves;
Your footsteps, as you tread the ground,
   The very grass with joy receives:
The innocence around your face
   All evil phantoms must repel;
Your heart is full of Nature's grace,
   Daisy-bell, sweet Daisy-bell.

   Daisy-bell, Daisy-bell,
When from the lips of childhood fell
The name that you have since retained,
And in your virtue never stained;
Say, did the sound suggest to you
   The thought to emulate that flower;
And keep your spirit pure and true,
   And stainless still from hour to hour?
Oh! let the lesson be your star,
   And ever in your bosom dwell;
Live worthy those whose hope you are;
   And be like them, sweet Daisy-bell.

MIDNIGHT.

Pass on, O wind! across the sea—
   The sky is dark, the night-clouds low—
My heart falls listening unto thee.

Thou dashest 'gainst my window-pane
  In sudden haste, and moaning loud,
To thy wild flight return'st again.

Like one who flies from shapes of dread,
  From memories of his guiltier years,
And clasps his hands behind his head;

Striving, all vainly, not to hear
  The groans of victims on his track;
And sees some sanctuary near,

And rushes to the unyielding door,
  But, gaining not the peace within,
Flies on in maddening haste once more.

Out on the dark, unfathomed sea,
  What deeds, O wind! were thine to-night?
What horror followeth after thee?

Crowded with shivering shapes of grief,
  What ships at thy approach have fled,
And dashed despairing on the reef?

What heart-wrung groans, what quick, sharp cries,
  What prayers for mercy and for grace
Have sped to-night through yonder skies?

Pass on, thou art a voice of fear—
  My heart is chilled, my blood is cold—
Pass on—thou hast no shelter here.

THE STAR IN THE WEST.

As I opened my eyes this morning,
  When the sun came over the hill,
I heard a quick tap at the window,
  And a twittering on the sill.

And a warble of exquisite sweetness,
   From a little bird outside the pane—
A little bird sitting and singing,
   Tapping and singing again.

And a wonderful fancy came o'er me—
   I thought 'twas your spirit I heard,
Your spirit, my love, come to call me
   In the shape of a beautiful bird ;
For to-day is the day I am coming
   To see you, my darling, again,
And I thought you were come to remind me,
   By tapping aloud at the pane.

Ah, love, you need never remind me,
   The days are too desolate far,
To cease to remember one moment
   The light of my beautiful star.
My beautiful star that is shining
   From her home far away in the west—
Where the seasons for ever are summer,
   And skies are the bluest and best.

But to-day is the day I am coming,
   (Oh would I already were there !)
My fingers will wander in rapture
   Through the gold-shining world of your hair.
My fingers will twine with your fingers,
   With their velvety, roseate tips,—
And my own will scarce breathe as I meet them,
   Those flower-soft, dew-lighted lips !

Ah, darling ! how sad have the days been !
   The desolate rain and the wind !
The clouds have been dark as in winter,
   And Nature like one stricken blind !

My heart has been darker than winter,
  Away from my star in the west ;
But to-night I shall lie like the lakelet,
  And she will drop down on my breast.

And out of the far-flowing future,
  What exquisite visions arise,
Of a time when I never shall wander
  Beyond the dear light of her eyes !
When her spirit shall never need call me
  From out her far home in the west ;
But she herself nestle for ever
  A beautiful bird in my breast !

THE OLD HAUNT.

O BREEZES from the sunny south
  Come, fan my fevered brow once more !
And bring from yon blue river's mouth
  Fresh sea-weed fragrance as of yore.
Come, frosting silvery lowland streams !
  Come, whitening upland slopes of wheat !
Companions of my early dreams,
  I hear your whispers at my feet.

Old rock whereon I pause to rest,
  Deep wrinkled with unnumbered years,
My cheek to thy rough cheek is pressed,
  Thy furrows channel blinding tears.
How oft, old rock, to grief unknown,
  I've climbed thy side in years gone by ;
And now, when utterly alone,
  I claim thy dumb, calm sympathy.

O grief! when most my visage daunts,
  When things most cherished fade and die,
How loathsome are our daily haunts,
  How sickening human sympathy !
I find more peace in this old rock,
  And in the breeze that o'er it strays,
Than years could bring with friends who mock
  My grief, by pointing brighter days.

I cool my brow against the stone,
  The dear old days before me glide :
Just now I started at the tone
  Of her sweet voice, here by my side.
God knows, perhaps the thought is weak,
  But I believe that this loved spot
Still hither draws her spirit meek,
  As *two* may come when I am not.

I feel her presence as I speak—
  A presence purer than the gold
Of evening on the mountain peak,
  Far o'er the earthward vapour's fold.
My pulses listen for her tread—
  My heart-strings cease their busy strife ;
Too well I feel 'tis I am dead,
  While she abides in perfect life.

EDWARD GEORGE KENT.

Tiie author of the following poems is a native of Lincolnshire, and at the age of seventeen published a volume full of promise, entitled " Nineveh, and other Poems." This was so well received by the public and the press, that the young author has completed arrangements to publish in 1861 a complete edition, illustrated, of his plays, poems, &c. Mr. Kent is the editor and proprietor of the " Christmas Yule Log," published annually, and a contributor to several provincial magazines.

TRUTHS OF LIFE.

Mournful truths I fain would utter,
　Truths of life that all must know,
Which the thoughtless lightly mutter,
　But the thoughtful really know.

We are living, wishing, waiting
　For great honours here to-day ;
But, alas ! to-morrow mating
　Others that have pass'd away.

Mighty cities, boasting nations,
　Sink before the shock of time ;
Quick-succeeding generations
　Muster at Death's awful chime !

He stands knocking, bidding, calling,
　All must satisfy his claim ;
Some like fruitless trees are falling,
　Worthless fuel for the flame.

Others, with no sense of sadness,
　At his stern command comply ;
'Tis to them a scene of gladness,
　And a glorious thing to die.

Life though sweet with all its treasures
   Cannot mitigate our doom;
Through its mingled toils and pleasures
   We are hastening to the tomb!

Let us, then, be up and ready,
   Every power of good unite,
In the battle firm and steady,
   Heaven will not withhold our right.

For the camp lights shine before us
   On the hills of love and peace;
Soon the struggle will o'ertake us,
   Soon the glimmering watchfire cease!

When this life with all its wonder,
   And this world with all its pain,
Shall be quickly rent asunder,
   May we at His right remain!

TO THE SKYLARK.

O SWEETEST songster of the skies,
   Could I, like thee, but yield a strain,
I then afar from earth would rise,
   And bid farewell to all its pain!
     And as the sun,
     At op'ning morn
       Uplights the busy earth,
     My song shall be
     Sweet minstrelsy
       And love's propitious birth.

O rapturous pilgrim of the clouds!
   Grant me thy joyous song,
That I may break these misty shrouds
   That round my spirit throng:

And view with glee
Those realms like thee,
　　Of never-changing love,
When thou ascend'st
To heaven, and blend'st
　　Thy voice with those above.

THE VAGRANT.

A LITTLE girl, with flaxen hair,
　　Stood singing in the street;
Her threadbare garments hung in rags,
　　Uncovered were her feet.

She sang a melancholy song;
　　A song of truth and woe—
" My mother's on her dying bed,
　　My father sleeps below.

" Good people, listen to my cry,
　　Give ear unto my prayer !"
But the heartless crowd still hurried by,
　　For none felt pity there.

Devoid of love, they could not read
　　That pleading, patient face,
And so, O dark and cruel deed,
　　They took her to that place—

Of mingled guilt and wretchedness,
　　Where thieves and drunkards slept;
And there, with no kind voice to bless,
　　The child that night was kept.

Poor child ! she struggled, but in vain,
　　She pleaded with her tears;
They heeded not her grievous pain,
　　Nor yet her youthful years !

Ere morn her mother's spirit wing'd
 Its heavenward angel-flight ;
These words upon her dying lips
 That sad and weary night :—

" Angels protect my hapless child,
 Wherever she may roam ;
And lead her through this night so wild
 In peace and safety home !"

God heard the pleading mother pray,
 And still'd her anxious breast ;
For lo ! before the break of day,
 Both were with Him, at rest !

THE BELFRY OF BOSTON.

NOBLE belfry, from thy chambers at the early blush of
 day
I beheld the rolling Witham wash thy basis in its
 spray ;

I beheld the evening shadows quit the scenes of coming
 morn,
Far away the verdant landscapes, and the fields of
 golden corn,

Lay enshrined in autumn's splendour, in the beams of
 solar light ;
When the dykes of fenny Holland seemed as veins of
 silver bright.

From thy mighty vaulted tower, mossy by the hand
 of time ;
Lo ! I heard the fleeting hour rung upon the iron
 chime.

From the old embattled turret, on thy topmost dizzy
    height,
I beheld the knavish jackdaw cut the air in speedy
    flight,

In the heavens far above me ; whilst the pilgrim of the
    sky
Sang the day's delightful dawning in sweet tones of
    melody.

I beheld in imaged fancy, tragic scenes from days of
    yore,
Scenes of murder, scenes of bloodshed, on the site of
    Lisbon's store :

Visions of the Spanish merchant, and his daughter fair
    and gay,
And the valiant knight of Cadiz, who seduced her
    heart away.

Preaching mendicants and friars, monks and military
    knights :
Followers of the great St. Francis and the lofty
    Eremites ;

Benedictine nuns of silence, silence sacred and severe,
From the busy world secluded, from its scenes of hope
    and fear.

Visions of the mournful cortége passing through the
    winding street,
To the ghostlike final dwelling where the high and
    lowly meet ;

Where the greatest of earth's children, ruling kingdoms
    with a breath,
Rival but the humblest peasant in the government of
    death.

Visions of the nuptial banquet, and the festivals of
  glee,
When Lord Hussey's noble towers rang with sounds of
  revelry.

Mighty men of former glory : noble men of ancient
  days,
Yet who live in history's record, pass'd before my
  early gaze,   .

While the tramp of mounted horsemen and the din of
  martial cries
Swept along the peopled borough, and arose unto the
  skies.

Yet I heard the sound of danger, and the sailors' cry at
  night,
With his shout of sudden gladness as he viewed thy
  form in sight ;

When the tolling of the sanctus, and the elevated
  lamp,
Flaming in thy world-fam'd lantern brought him to his
  homely camp.

While the bustling of the borough, and the whistling
  of the train,
Bore me through the mist of ages to the scenes of
  yore again.

As I view'd the dead around thee, in death's sacred,
  solemn trust,
Then I breathed a silent blessing on our fathers'
  honour'd dust ;

Who upreared thee, noble temple, not for worshippers
  of wood,
Nor the bowl of burning incense, nor the sacrifice of
  blood !

But a court of greater glory, and a monument that
    bears
The story of their noble work throughout the stress of
    years.

But oppressive feeling thrilled me as I view'd those
    towers no more ;
Towers cast down by wars and pillage, buried with the
    pomp of yore.

They with chantries of rich income, and the castles of
    renown,
Have succumbed to age's quarrel, yet thou lookest o'er
    the town.

While the bridge across the river long has ceased to
    jar and creak,
And no more St. Botolph's pikemen for the fierce
    marauders shriek.

All the monasterial power and the convent's might is
    lost,
And their old mysterious records long have mouldered
    in the dust.

All the pomp of glorious Tilney, with the pride of
    Rochford 's fled,
Long their motley followers have slumbered with the
    dead ;

Yet thou standst the same unalter'd proof against the
    threats of time,
In defiance of his power ; noble structure ! work
    sublime !

Yet thou standst a pile of honour, noblest tower in the
    fen,
Relic of departed ages ; relic of departed men !

Whlie I stood upon thy belfry, echoes from the busy
    square
Turned my thoughts to worldly fancies, all my visions
    into air:

As the hour had now departed duty summon'd me
    away,
O'er thy form of might and grandeur fell the open blaze
    of day.

HUMAN LIFE.

I FANCIED on the bridge of life I stood:
    Beneath its arch I saw the human tide
Flow on with Time in its eventful flood.
    I saw upon its surf a child and guide;
Its guide was Truth, who held its fairy form
    In safety from the wildness of the stream,
Girt in true wisdom, proof against the storm,
    While passing o'er it sung a noble theme.
I look'd again, when, lo, an earthly god
    Appeared, while hundreds in his train he bore,
Each in their hands upheld a golden rod;
    And lo! at once they sank to rise no more.
I now thought I was struggling in the stream,
But, glad surprise! I found 'twas but a dream.

PRIDE.

O MAN! behold the starry vault, or look
    At Nature's pencil in the lovely flower;
Survey the ocean or the crystal brook,
    Or smell the perfume of the fragrant bower.

Think of the Maker of them all, sublime;
 Remember He's the same who made the worm
That crawls unseen, the constant friend of Time,
 The ruthless waster of thy lowly form.
I say, 'tis He who for just purpose made
 Thee but of dust; where is thy might and pride?
Think not of beauty, which in time will fade,
 Or gold, which all ere long must lay aside;
Divest thyself of all such empty show,
Thy Maker learn, thy feeble nature know.

POEMS BY G. I. F.

WE feel much pleasure in accepting the following contributions. Their touching simplicity and earnestness sufficiently prove that the sentiments expressed by the writer are genuine. The poem "Anna Garibaldi" exhibits great promise, and deserves to be better known.

THE TWO ANGELS.

(FROM THE GERMAN OF GEIBEL.)

TELL me, my heart, if thou dost know
The sister-angels here below—
 In Heaven their seat?
On Friendship's brow the lily blows,
And Love bears high the fragrant rose,
 Her emblem meet.

Black are Love's locks, like fire she glows;
Beauteous as spring, which budding goes
 O'er vale and hill:
Mild Friendship blooms in softer light,
And she is like the summer night,
 So soft and still!

Love on the lightning-flash descends,
While Friendship with the moonbeam blends
   Her glimmering ray;
Love comes to conquer and possess,
But Friendship gives itself no less,
   When none repay.

Love is a sea where tempests rave,
And wave beats ceaseless upon wave,
   In tumult wild.
Friendship, a lake so clear and deep,
That Heaven, reflected there, doth keep
   Its image mild.

Thrice happy, and thrice truly blest,
The heart where Love turns in to rest
   For ever bright.
And where the glow upon the rose
Tends not to wither, but disclose
   The lily's light!

RETURN.

By thy vows in secret spoken,
By thine ever-cherished token,
   Return and press me to thy beating heart;
By those words, which on the shore,
Mingled with the ocean's roar,
   Return, return, and never more to part.

By the happy, mystic hour,
When first we felt Love's boundless power,
   Return and press me to thy throbbing breast;
For oh! my heart is restless as the ocean,
Till thou return and still its motion,
   In vain I seek to lull it into rest!

Return, and sorrow shall for ever flee,
Return, for thou art all the world to me;
Return, for night is day when thou 'rt away,
Return, and night shall turn to endless day!

———◆———

ANNA GARIBALDI.

" Awake, Anita, wake again,
   All is not lost so thou remain,
      Thou lady of my soul!
   Awake, else shall my guilt be great,
   Who brought thee from thy peaceful state,
      To where war's thunders roll.

" In vain I plead—thy pulse is stayed,
   Thy head upon the arm is laid,
      That fain would rest with thee :
   But it must labour, dare, and toil,
   Nor pause, till that thrice-sacred soil
      Which holds thee, shall be free.

" From San Marino came the foe,
   Our fragile barks sped down the Po,
      T'wards Adriatic's wave;
   But ere we reached Venetia's strand
   Thou sought'st for health upon the land,
      And found a grave!

" Thy tottering steps I onward bore
   From Mesolé's too open shore,.
      To forest shades opaque;
   There, though I sought it all around,
   No drop of water could be found
      Thy dying thirst to slake.

" Alas ! heart-broken and forlorn
I may not linger here and mourn,
　My country bids me rise :
Could I but see her people free,
My only further aim would be
To join thee in the skies."

Thus Garibaldi spake ; his thoughts the while
Fled over ocean's ever-restless main,
And through the chequered wilderness of life,
And rested on those regions of the west
Where first he felt the power of Love, and knew
Himself beloved.　And then, as thought knows not
The bounds of space and time, in Future's realm
(That undiscovered world, whose entrance, man
Nor angel is allowed to penetrate),
His fancy wrought a vision beautiful :
Lo ! where Italia, underneath a sky
Of deepest blue, brought forth her olive boughs,
Fit emblem of the peace that reigned around ;
And over all there brooded with outspread
Protecting wings, the Angel Liberty !
The spirits sent to guard each mortal's soul
Sang hymns of praise, and angels round the Throne,
Took up the strain.
　　　　　　　　Oh, welcome as the branch
Which pierced the waters that once hid the world,
Welcome as freedom to the prisoner dove,
When from the ark she flew and came no more,
So welcome, through the impenetrable mist
That hid the Future (as the waters, earth),
Did Garibaldi see that vision rise.
He knew it, a presentiment of good,
Offspring of Hope, and that strange sympathy
Which mortals feel with that which is to be.

Meanwhile, the messenger of Death flew up
To Heaven—and, as he may not enter there,
He laid his precious burden at the gates.
When they unclose, Life at the portal waits,
And with a close embrace shall gently guide
All ransomed spirits to the realms of bliss.

THE OWL.

ALL in the darkness of the night,
The mournful owlet takes its flight,
   A harbinger of woe.
Hark to its oft-repeated cry,
Now far away, and now more nigh;
   To-who! to-who! to-who!

Tell me, thou melancholy bird,
Is it a warning I have heard,
   From Death, and must I go?
Art thou a messenger of his?
And dost thou tell me that he is
   A foe! a foe! a foe!

One dread struggle ends the strife,
When Death shall lead me to a life
   Where no more tears shall flow.
Is he a foe shall bring me there?
I hear thee answer through the air
   Oh no! oh no! oh no!

THE LOST ONE.

OH, he was fair!
   More beautiful than words can tell!
And on his hair,
   The golden hues of sunset fell.

Oh, he was dear!
  Much more beloved than words can tell!
To have him near
  Was happiness no grief could quell.

And when he died,
  (Oh, grief too deep for words to tell!)
All nature cried,
  And every heart sent up a knell.

On that blest shore,
  Whose joys no eloquence can tell,
For evermore
  We trust that he is gone to dwell!

—◦◦—

WHAT IS LOVE?

KNOWING well, to us impart
What thou knowest, oh my heart!
And tell me what is Love?
" *Two* souls so closely bound,
That but *one* thought is found.
Two hearts whose union sweet,
Needs but one single beat;
This, this alone is Love."

And say, whence doth this Love appear?
" I only know that it is here."
And where doth Love when fled, repose?
" That is not Love, it never goes."
And when is Love the purest—best?
" When thoughts of self are laid at rest.
Where may the deepest Love be found?
" When silent, it emits no sound."
Say how the richest Love is known?
" 'Tis richest when it gives its own."
And how Love speaks, I fain would know?
" It doth not speak, it loveth so."

LINES FOR AN ALBUM.
(FROM THE GERMAN.)

OH! could I with fair flowers twine
True happiness, it should be thine;
Whole wreaths I'd bind, with anxious care,
That every blessing should be there!

———◆◇◆———

BIRTHDAY VERSES TO PHILIP.

JUST thirteen years have passed away,
Dear Philip, since the happy day
   That thou wert born:
Thou cam'st to us in summer-hours,
A blossom, 'mid the blooming flowers
   That deck'd the lawn!

The July flowers so bright and fair,
Shedding sweet perfume through the air,
   Too soon they die!
And in the fading light of day,
How beautiful the sun's last ray,
   Gleams in the sky!

But brighter than the flow'rs thine eyes,
And sweeter incense ne'er can rise
   Than words of pray'r!
Dearer to us than evening rays,
The never-fading light that plays
   Upon thy hair!

Farewell! may many happy years
Laden with smiles, unwash'd by tears,
   Upon thee shine!
With lowly heart and ready hand,
Haste onward, to the Promised Land,
   May it be thine!

WILLIAM STOKES.

THE author of the following extracts from a volume entitled "The Olive-Branch" (London: Judd and Glass,) is a native of Purfleet, on the banks of the Thames, but now a citizen of Manchester. The poems, chiefly of a political character, are many of them exceedingly beautiful, and sufficiently prove the author to be, not only an earnest writer, but in sympathy with all that is good and true. This very pretty little volume has afforded us great pleasure, and both it and its author deserve to be better known; and we trust in future volumes to renew our acquaintance with the fruits of his hours with the Muses. Mr. Stokes is the author of several successful Essays, as well as the volume already noticed.

THE FREEMAN'S SONG.

O GIVE me the freedom to speak as I think,
And liberty's fulness with Milton to drink ;—
To bask on the mountain, or bathe in the stream,
To wander with sages—with poets to dream!

O give me the freedom to utter and teach
The heartfelt conviction in plain, open speech;
With Cato, and Hampden, and Chatham to stand,
And plead with all boldness the weal of my land!

O give me the freedom to make honest search,
For sect and for party, for creed and for church ;—
To act for myself in all matters divine,
Nor " soundings " to take with " another man's line !"

O give me the freedom to stand forth alone,
And vice to expose, though the vice of the throne ;
Nor let me be shackled, or fettered, or fined,
When stringing my bow at the faults of mankind!

O give me the freedom and home of the brave,
With soil never trod by the foot of the slave;
Where tyrants, and dungeons, and chains are unknown,
And liberty's smile is the stay of the throne!

O give me this treasure!—then perish the gold,
That miser-fools barter for liberty sold!
I'll rove on the mountain, the broad ocean scan,
And sing the lov'd freedom that makes me a man.

INVOCATION TO THE SPIRIT OF PEACE.

COME over the mountain, come over the sea,
Thou First-born of heaven, thou Pride of the free!
Come fresh on the morning, with wings of the dove,
And strew in thy passage the blessings of love.

Appear in thy radiance, thou Angel of light,
And chase from creation the gloom of the night;
Disperse the thick shadows that over us spread,
And be to all nations as life from the dead.

Drive back to their caverns the dark hosts of death,
And scatter the forces of war with thy breath;
Proclaim to the world a new era begun,
And let it be lasting as light from the sun.

In broad open day show the scroll of the dead,
And let it by heroes and monarchs be read;
And give them to blush for the guilt of the hour,
That made war and bloodshed the " balance of power."

Array to their vision the souls of the slain,
With heartbroken widows and orphans in train:
Tear off the disguise from their " glory " and pride,
And ask what they show for the men who have died.

N

Before them display, in its ruin and fire,
Some Kertch or Canton, with the woe of the sire;
Then, pointing to wealth spent in battle and flame,
Demand what they give in return—but a name.

Proclaim that the Judge of the quick and the dead
Will "make inquisition for blood" they have shed;
Yet turn far away heavy judgments in store,
If, mourning their folly, they "learn war no more."

Thus come, gentle Peace, fix thy reign upon earth,
And bring the glad day of the world's second birth:
"The bow in the cloud," when dark thunder-storms
    cease,
Be thou to creation, sweet Spirit of Peace!

----◦◦----

THE ANGEL OF PEACE.

RING, ring the sweet bells, and unfurl the gay banners!
    Let cold party-feeling and enmity cease;
Arise, ye glad nations, with lofty hosannahs!
    And welcome with triumph the Angel of Peace.

Long, long have the foemen dealt fury around them;
    Too long spread the flame of destruction and death;
Too long has the demon of discord spell-bound them,
    And blasted the hope of the world with his breath.

Sing, sing the loud chorus! his spell is now broken,
    And nations once more breathe the air of the free;
His watchword of " glory " shall henceforth be spoken,
    To die with the echo that floats on the sea.

For, dove-like, the angel has passed o'er the waters,
    And wept when he saw but a deluge of blood;
His olive-branch waved o'er the scene of the slaughters,
    And Peace spread her " bow " on the face of the
        flood.

Then sing! for the ark safely rests on the mountain,
  The crimson-dyed waters haste, blushing, away ;
The sun gilds afresh both the stream and the fountain,
  And man hails with rapture the smile of the day.

Then join the loud chorus! unfurl the gay banners!
  Let peace be the watchword the universe o'er ;
Unite, all ye nations, in lofty hosannahs!
  And sing, " Peace our glory!" and " Peace ever-
    more!"

TO THE ISLE OF MAN.

THOU gem of the Ocean, thou pearl of the Sea,
Whose rock-begirt shores are the Home of the Free ;
Thou Queen among Islands, though small thy domain,
I love thy fair sceptre, and leave thee with pain.

Full oft have I roamed o'er thy native delights,
Thy soft-flowing dells, or thy cloud-crested heights ;
Or sooth'd by the " Douglas," have follow'd the stream,
Where lovers may whisper, or poets may dream.

And each rolling season that gives me once more
To view thy bold outline and tread thy sweet shore ;
Endears thee anew, like some friend, to my heart,
From whom it may never, no, never depart.

For what though the haughty and proud may disdain,
To bow to thy sceptre and hallow thy reign ;
What though giddy fashion may seek other skies,
Thou hast, O fair Mona! a lovelier prize.

Oh Labour! thou Nurse of our national Health,
Thou spring-head of Commerce, and parent of Wealth!
Thou glory of Britain,—thy children, when free,
Are lovely as Princes to Mona and me.

Where'er in the day of their freedom they roam,
Their smiles spread around them the Englishman's
    home ;
And no gilded coronet graces the soil,
Like the bold manly forms of these children of toil.

Upon thy fair bosom, thou gem of the West!
Long, long may these thousands be welcome, and blest;
And be it thy glory, wherever they roam,
That Mona can find them an Englishman's Home.

LITTLE JENNY.

I sat on the stile by the rich waving corn,
And drank the sweet air in the pride of the morn ;
The lark broke from slumbers and soar'd beyond sight,
But pour'd ceaseless music from regions of light.

A prim little maiden came tripping along,
And sweet was her blue eye, but sweeter her song ;
She glanced at the stranger,—her look seemed to say,
" Sir, let me pass over nor hinder my way."

That look was a study, and spoke of her haste,
Unconscious that maiden of guile or of " taste ;"
Her ringlets of auburn flowed wild on the air,
And innocence reigned on that countenance fair.

I said, " Little maiden, you're happy to-day,
You sing as yon lark which is soaring away ;"
" O yes, Sir," she answered, " I cannot be sad,
With so much around me to make my heart glad.

" Yon cottage you see by the side of the hill,
With the woodbine around it and close by the rill,
That, Sir, is my home—and no home is so fair,
For father, and mother, and baby are there."

" But, maiden, your cottage looks humble and low,
'Tis not like the mansion you passed on that brow ;
That mansion is large, and its rooms are so fine,
A palace, compared to that cottage of thine."

" O Sir," said the maiden, " no stranger can tell,
What sweetness resides in the home where I dwell ;
That mansion is larger and finer to see,
Yet never can equal that cottage to me.

" My father he loves me, and I love him too,
He often says, ' Jenny, a warm kiss for you ;'
And mother, she speaks in a language so mild,
And calls me her Jenny, her own little child.

" And baby,—his name, Sir, is Johnny, you know,—
He also is happy and smiles at me too ;
And when mother tells me to give him his food,
He looks like an angel, so sweet, and so good.

" O Sir, I do think you are wrong when you say,
My cottage is not like that mansion so gay ;
No mansion is like it, no palace so fair,
When father, and mother, and baby are there."

I saw I had touch'd a sad chord in her heart,
And said, " Little maiden, before you depart,
I tell you you're right, and wherever you roam,
No place will you love like that sweet cottage home.

" Yon mansion looks down on that humble hill side,
And wears a bold front as it frowns in its pride ;
But, maiden, the humble, content with their lot,
Find heaven on earth in the lowliest cot."

"O yes, Sir," she said, as she curtsied away,
" My father and mother have taught me to pray ;
And often they tell me that life when well spent,
Will make any cottage the home of content."

,

J. A. LANGFORD.

THE author of the following beautiful poems is already known to a large circle of poetical readers, having published an anonymous volume of great merit, entitled "The Lamp of Life," and subsequently " Poems of the Field and Town," "Shelley," &c. &c. The "Leader," in reviewing Mr. Langford's last efforts, observes: " The occasional poems are fair samples of lyric effort, and all are marked with a melody of utterance which gives pleasure to attention, and cheers the critic's labour. The poet's talent lies in the reflective direction as well as in the descriptive. He can penetrate the dim-discovered tracts of mind, as well as the open champaign of cultivated nature." From many of Mr. Langford's poems we have derived great pleasure: they are full of delightful thoughts, elegantly, earnestly, and musically expressed.

Mr. Langford's last volume, entitled "Shelley," (London: Smith, Elder, and Co.,) from which we make the extracts entitled "Italy," distinguishes its author as a poet of no mean capacity.

ITALY.

ITALIA, O Italia! thou hast been,
And art, the land to every pilgrim dear;
To thee he turns as to his own heart's Queen,
When sorrow needs some lovely thing to cheer.
Thy very name's a charm which exiles hear
With rapture, conjuring up the hour
When greatness was thy playmate; grace severe
Sat on thy brow; and earth confessed thy power;
And beauty then as now was aye thy fatal dower.

O land of Art and Song!   Poor chastened one!
The soil where tyrants play their bloody game,
Yet cannot rob thee of thy glories, won
By painter and by poet; for thy fame

Is as a quenchless, still-ascending flame,
And soars beyond the malice, hatred, rage
Of puny despots, whose careers of shame
Shall be the bywords of a coming age,
While thy beloved name will aye men's love engage.

And beautiful as beauty's self thou art:
Adorned with every charm and every grace
That sunny skies, bright hills, and lakes impart.
The richest works of Nature find a place
Upon thy fruitful bosom; rivers trace
Their murmurous courses through the vine-clad plain,
Where winding tendrils fondly interlace
To bear their glowing burdens, whence men strain
The ruby-tinted wine to gladden heart and brain.

The land of beauty and of bondage too;
The land of untold glory and of shame;
The land whence poets inspiration drew,
And dowered with all their never-dying fame.
The land of deathless memories which inflame
The living with the hope of nobler days,
When Liberty again his home shall claim,
And win once more earth's benison and praise,
Once more be crowned with green as well as faded bays."

THE MARTYR'S PREPARATION.

FROM THE "DEATH OF ST. POLYCARP."

Long time he prayed.
For two rich hours his spirit left the earth,
And held communion with God. His voice,
So often exercised in prayer and praise,
Serener rose in this his peril time,
Than when in safety and in peace. His foes,
Made callous by repeated wrongs, grew mild,

And listened wond'ringly, that one so old,
Surrounded by the messengers of death,
And threatened with a fierce and cruel end,
Could thus forget himself. He prayed for all:
The weak, the groaning, persecuted Church—
The poor, afflicted brethren in the faith—
His foes, who raged, not knowing what they did.
He prayed for all; and, lastly, for himself:
For strength to bear whatever pain and shame
The rage of frenzied fancy could suggest,
The cruelty of savage hearts inflict;
For thus sustained all suffering would be bliss,
And he should die rejoicingly; should pass
With prayer upon his tongue, smiles on his lips;
Nor bring disgrace upon the infant faith,
Nor prove unworthy of his Lord and Christ.
        Then calmly came the old man forth. His face
Shone gloriously bright; and from his eyes
A heavenly splendour beamed. E'en so of old
The favoured Moses looked, when from the fire
Upon Mount Sinai's height he turned
And gazed upon the people. So looked he:
But all the terror softened and subdued
Into a sweet, celestial grace, which told
That Sinai's thunders, Sinai's law, no more
Came threatening unto man; but in their stead
The blessed Gospel sealed upon the cross:
The burden light of mercy, faith, and grace.
So calmly came the old man forth—no shout,
No cry of loud, exulting foes—no sign
Of gratified revenge—now greeted him.
In silence the proconsul's soldiers came
And met him; placed him on an ass; and thus,
As rode the Holy One, but without pomp
Of gladdened maidens strewing flowers along,
Or loud hosannas singing as they went,
The fond disciple journeyed to his doom.

MY OWN.

SHE is no proud and stately dame,
  Of high imperial mien;
She looks not her admirers down,
  A self-elected queen.
Her brow by Nature ne'er was made
  A diadem to bear;
Nor would a coronet adorn
  Her freely-flowing hair.

She is a light and airy thing,
  A girl of love and grace;
And tenderness beams in her eye,
  And health smiles in her face.
She moves about, a joy to see,
  As noiseless as a bird;
And when she sings from lark or thrush
  No sweeter strains are heard.

I wooed her well, and wooed her long;
  And yet she was so shy,
Whene'er I prayed her love, she said,
  " I'll answer by-and-by."
When violets sweetened first the Spring,
  And when the corn was brown,
I pleaded warmly for her " Yes "—
  Love's hope, and end, and crown.

And now she moves about *our* home,
  Or sits beside *our* fire,
Or, smiling, meets me at the door,
  Whence worldly cares retire:
Is still the same light airy thing,
  No sweet attraction flown,
But graced with one, the crown of all,
  For she is now—MY OWN.

THE FIRST KISS.

THE stars have never shone so bright;
   The night was never so divine;
And ne'er o'er such a silent sea
   Did harvest moon so yellow shine.
And in our boat we glided on,
   And watched the waters silently:
Old Ocean's fire-flies sparkled round,
   And rivalled Heaven's own galaxy.

The softest breath of Autumn air,
   Our naked foreheads fanned and kist;
And far away on shore we saw
   Fond lovers keeping lovers' tryst.
And on the stars we, silent, gazed;
   And gazed upon the silent sea;
And watched the lovers far away,
   And wondered if they loved like we.

We spoke not: but we felt the love
   The tongue in vain attempts to say;
And gazing silently on all,
   Our hearts in love's deep silence lay.
'Twas then, o'ercome by Beauty's charm,
   O'ercome by Love's heart-moving power,
Thy blushing lips first pressed on mine,
   And sanctified that glorious hour.

Oh blessëd night! Its memory
   Is sweet and precious to me now:
Again I see its moon and stars,
   And feel its breath upon my brow.
Again those fire-flies round me glow;
   I see the lovers in their bliss;
But sweeter far, I feel once more
   Upon my lips thy first fond kiss.

FRANK NORMAN.

Mr. Norman has recently published a very creditable volume of "Poems," (London: Ward and Lock,) which deserves to be better known. A reviewer in the "Critic" observes: "Mr. Norman seems to have quite a gift for song-writing, some of which strike us as by no means unworthy of Haynes Bayly, or even of Moore."

TO THE MUSE.

Sweet Poesy, I come again
   To thee with yearning breast,
Beguile away that secret pain
   My bosom's phantom-guest!

No aid like thine when anxious care
   The soul is bowing down,
To bid the smiles of peace appear
   And cancel every frown!

My boyhood and my youth have felt
   Thine omnipresent aid,
No sorrow in my heart has dwelt
   Which thou hast not allayed.

I would not care to live, when song
   Has still'd upon my breath,
Oh! if the dream must break ere long,
   Let it but break in Death!

STANZAS.

Oh! why must Childhood's happy dreams,
   Like Spring's fresh flow'rs, so early fade?
Why flee the bliss-born golden beams
   That once in Youth the earth array'd?

Why must the shadowy forms of care
  Like spectres in Life's pathway rise?
Why pass so soon those seasons fair
  Which made a heaven beneath the skies?

I know not—but I feel 'twere sweet
  To die before these dreams are o'er,—
And pass to those we yearn to meet
  Upon an amaranthine shore!

For oh! too oft we love the spell
  Which consecrates an early love,
And find the dream we lov'd so well
  And thought so sweet, can bitter prove!

———◆———

LOVE AND AFFECTION.

AWAY, thou tempter garbed in bliss,
Whose dart may be a maiden's kiss,
With pleasure ever in thy breath
And many a fatal snare beneath!
Away, enchanting one! I know
What thou dost oftentimes bestow.

Away! thy voice is not for those
Who once have plucked the blooming rose,
And then beheld its beauties fade,
Its fragrance lost, its smile decay'd.
Oh! Love, though like an angel drest
Leave, leave me and my heart at rest.

But thou, Affection, treasure given
To lead us nearer unto heaven—
Whilst Love's strong frenzy rageth wild,
Dwell with me like some angel-child,
Constant and passionless remain,
For Love is but a name for Pain.

THE DYING SWAN.

ABOVE the murmuring waters, sweet
    The zephyr bears along—
Re-echoed from each wild retreat
    A slow and mournful song.

A lay from melting sadness caught
    That charms the listening ear,
So wild a melody—yet fraught
    With music soft and clear.

As if with unseen wings, that strain
    A life seems bearing on,
Whilst in Death's agonizing pain
    Bewails the dying swan.

The soul of Music erewhile bound
    Within its bosom, yields to Death,
And now breaks forth in plaintive sound,
    Its farewell failing breath.

And thus in notes as sweet as those
    Of dying swan, would I,
When Death's deep shadows round me close,
    Sing sweetest, and then die!

Miscellaneous.

THE SMILE UPON MY HOME.

THESE and the following verses, entitled " Life's Reaper," are by
J. H. Jewell, who has written several ballads for which music has
been successfully adapted.

IN ev'ry tone of music
    Thy silv'ry voice I hear;
In ev'ry phase of beauty
    Thy form is still more dear.
In the first blush of morning
    With sunbeams smiling bright,
Thy face seems beaming o'er me
    A glimpse of angel light.
In hours of rest and silence
    What happy visions come!
I feel that thou art near me
    To smile upon my home.

Thus all around me beameth
    With smiling joys and rays
Of sunny, happy moments,
    Bring bright and holy days.
More near to me than ever
    Thy spirit seems to come,
To cheer me with its presence
    To smile upon my home.

LIFE'S REAPER.

MOTHER, when the spring flowers came
    And I was pale and ill,
You bade me place my trust, and bow
    Unto my Maker's will.
You said, when sober autumn deckt
    Her fields with golden grain,
My cheek would wear the cheering glow
    Of joyous health again.

" Mother, the summer's sun has made
    The flowers to spring and bloom,
And yet I feel each glorious morn
    Much nearer to the tomb.
I've lived to see the autumn time,
    And hope fades with my tears ;
I cannot reach the harvest-field
    To glean the scatter'd ears."

" My child," the weeping mother said,
    " Kind Providence will deign
To garner thee as husbandmen
    Now garner in their grain.
He wills that we should bring forth fruit,
    Meet for repentance here,
That when his ripening harvest comes
    Death's sickle will be near."

Night came, the harvest-moon threw forth
    Its silver-tinted light ;
The flick'ring spirit of the child
    Seem'd eager for its flight.
The reaper, Death, came when the moon
    Shone out in bright array ;
But when his shadow passed, the child's
    Blest spirit fled away.

THE FISHER'S WIFE.

By John Harris, author of " Lays," &c., " The Land's End, Kynance Cove," &c., " The Mountain Prophet, The Mine, and other Poems."

" Look through the lattice, Laura,
   Look out upon the main :
'Tis time your fisher father
   Was at his home again.
The winds are wailing wildly,
   The great waves lash the strand :
O Saviour, save the fisher,
   And bring him safe to land !"

And Laura through the casement
   Gazed o'er the sand-hills brown
Upon the fretted ocean,
   Which rolled in fury down.
No vessel met her vision,
   Or boat, upon the blue,
But hills of foamy water,
   And clouds of pitchy hue.

" Look, look again, my Laura :
   How fast comes on the night !
O what a sheet of lightning
   Is blazing round the height !
The pent-up rains are falling,
   The thunders meet in strife :
O, when will come the fisher,
   The sunshine of my life ?"

And Laura's eyes are gleaming
   Again upon the sea ;
No boat is seen approaching,
   Or fisher on the quay.

The sun has sunk in shadow,
  A thick black darkens space—
Her heart beats hard and harder
  And tears are on her face.

" Now trim the midnight taper
  And, Laura, let us creep
Together to the doorway,
  And back again to weep.
The storm is raging louder,
  And deeper moans the sea ;
The dismal darkness thickens ;
  No fisher comes to me."

And when the blush of morning
  Hung on the bright'ning air,
They early sought the seaside,
  To weep in sorrow there.
For one a sire and lover,
  And one a husband found,
Wash'd dead upon the shingles—
  The fishermen were drowned.

You see that cottage yonder ;
  The thatch is old and gray :
There Laura and her mother
  Are living to this day.
And one is fresh as summer,
  One wintry, reft, and riven ;
And both wear weeds of widowhood,
  And both prepare for heaven.

A CHILD'S PRAYER.

THIS and the two following—"Pain" and "The Rainbow"—are by W. R. Evans, author of "A Century of Fables," a very pretty, entertaining, and clever book of translations and adaptations. It consists of the Flowers of Fable from the literature of many nations; for its author is an accomplished linguist, as well as a scholar of good taste. We are proud to remember that Mr. Evans is a self-taught working man; but sorry to hear that his first volume, although so highly commended, has not been very remunerative. He is, we understand, about to publish a new volume by subscription, which, we trust, will compensate for his outlay. Prospectuses of the new work may be obtained from the author, 40, Seymour Street, Euston Square, London.

A LITTLE girl scarce five years old
　Grew sick well-nigh to death ;
And, lying in her little cot,
　Drew heavily her breath.

Her mother, watching by the couch,
　Knelt down at times to pray,
And mutely begg'd God would not take
　Her little one away.

And while she thought her treasure slept,
　Grown earnest with her grief,
She gently murmur'd once a prayer,
　To give her soul relief.

But still the child half-dozing lay
　Upon her tiny bed,
And overheard in silent awe
　Much that the suppliant said.

Then, as her parent rose again,
　She said in earnest tone :
"O mother, do you think that I
　Must go to heaven alone?"

" Alone, my pet! nay, say not so;
  For the good God is there,
And round about his golden throne
  Are angels mild and fair."

" But, mother," said the little one,
  " I should not like to leave
You, father, and my sisters dear,
  And all my friends, to grieve."

" Dear child," the weeping mother said,
  " I would not have you go;
But yet God's holy will be done,
  If He hath will'd it so.

" He'll be your Father up on high;
  In Christ a friend you'll find;
His mother Mary will be yours,
  The seraphs, sisters kind."

" But still," replied the innocent,
  " Their faces would be strange:
I know you all, and love you so,
  I do not wish to change.

" I'll pray to God to let me stay,
  To learn a great deal more
Of Him and heaven, and let me come
  When you have gone before."

Think not these infant words profane:
  That prayer was heard above;
The child grew well, and daily learnt
  To know the God of love.

And when in after-years again
  On dying-bed she lay,
No mother watching by her then,
  She pray'd she might not stay.

PAIN.

THANK Heaven for this returning pain,
That warneth me to rest again!
" Thank Heaven for pain!" some sufferer cries,
And lifts his brows in rash surprise.
But think a while, impatient man :
Learn, all is good in Nature's plan
But our own souls ; for these alone
Are free to err, and aye have shown
That those who blame their Maker's rule
Are powerless their own breasts to school.

    Thank Heaven for pain! the warning sign
That monisheth of health's decline,
And Nature's struggle to insure,
With man's own aid, a speedy cure.
Thank Heaven for pain! let all men cry,
Who value life, or fear to die.
Let pain be banish'd from the earth,
And what were man's existence worth ?
How fiends would dance, and Death would grin,
To see the fell disease within
Slow sapping all the life away,
While man went careless on and gay,
Unconscious of his coming doom
Until he trod upon his tomb.

    Thank Heaven for pain! that daily saves
Its thousands from untimely graves ;—
An angel-messenger—nay, more ;
For angels were sent down of yore
To warn mankind, and spoke in vain
To those who would have heeded pain.

    Yea, greater wonders pain hath wrought
Than all that wisest men have taught :
And while it makes the body whole,
Proves oft a purger of the soul.

The prodigal, whose health and years
Were squander'd, while a mother's tears
And father's counsels vainly fell,
Hath oft obey'd its potent spell.
  Pain as a teacher first appears,
Appealing to man's hopes and fears;
Next as a judge, severe and stern
To him who may refuse to learn;
And should he wilfully despise
The earlier, gentler penalties,
And reformation still defer,
Pain turneth executioner;
But yet in mercy it invites
To penitence the while it smites,
And often proveth even then
A minister of good to men:
Who mock'd it as a judge, at least
May, dying, hear it as a priest.

THE RAINBOW.

FROM THE GERMAN OF RÜCKERT.

WHERE on earth the rainbow resteth,
  Stands a golden chalice bright:
He that goes there may behold it,
  Clear and radiant to the sight.

With a wine of heaven that chalice
  E'er is full and brimming o'er;
He that haply drinketh of it,
  Suffereth from thirst no more.

Hither, thither, late and early,
  Have I sought the radiant spot
Where on earth the rainbow resteth;
  But attain it could I not.

Never, never could I reach it,—
Never taste the heavenly wine :
Still unquench'd within me burneth,
Still will burn this thirst of mine.

WEAK THINGS.

(1 Cor. i. 27, 28.)

BY EDWARD SWAINE.

SCORN ye earth's weak ones?   Her weak things, in
    warning —
Vines as they cluster, and streams as they flow,
Mists robed in beauty—reprove the proud scorning,
    Crying, " Beware how ye frown on the low !"

Is there not life in the vine for thy fainting ?
    Will not the streamlet, in thirst, make thee bow ?
Shall not the cloud which the rose-light is painting,
    Teach thee to blush for thy scorn of the low ?

See ! the land darkens, and earthquakes are rocking ;
    " Finished " redemption and Hell's overthrow—
Tell who the victor ?   The same they are mocking ;
    Lo ! 'tis the LORD, while they count Him the *low !*

Scorn ye no more—the best blessings that shower
    Wrap them where thoughts of the proud never go :
So, in their time, may the weak rise in power,
    So may the haughty be helped by the low !

SAD MEMORIES,

BY E. W. HUDDLESTON, a young native of Manchester, many of whose contributions to our last volume were greatly admired. We hope next year to be favoured with others from his pen.

OFT in passionate appealing,
    Oft in love-congealing hate,
 Oft in smiles despair concealing,   .
    Broken-hearted, desolate,
Have I wrestled with my sorrow,
    Yet my tears unbidden flow;
Doth the unrevealed to-morrow
    Any hidden solace know?

Sitting musing o'er the olden
    Beauties of the passed-away,
Memory-litten, lives the golden
    Radiance of evanished day;
Gazing on the flickering glories
    Panorama'd on the wall,
Listening to the ancient stories
    Murmuring through the lonely hall;—

Silvery songs from harping angels,
    Silent looks from saintly eyes,
Faltering tones, Hope's faint evangels,
    Whispers floating from the skies;
Dim and dreamy ghosts immortal,
    Flit before my trembling eye,
All that issues from the portal
    Of a lifelong memory!

Many treasured tendernesses,
    Souvenirs of the bliss of yore—
Faded blossoms, silken tresses,
    Clinging memories, evermore

Breathing of the blighted maiden
   Whom I loved in days gone by ;
Thoughts of all things anguish-laden
   Hover here continually.

Ever in my spirit burneth
   Fierce and unattained desire,
For the peace that ne'er returneth—
   Who shall still this quenchless fire ?
Is there in the cloudy morning
   Aught serene behind the veil ?
Must I ever deem in scorning
   Hope a mere imagined tale ?

Shall a joy-sun's vivid shining
   Sorrow's dew exhale in tears ?
Banish all the bitter pining,
   Conquer all the woes of years ?
Questioning, but answered never,
   Save by echoes, still must I
Wander wearily for ever
   Pondering on Memory !

IN AFFLICTION.

ALTHOUGH we have entitled our volume a collection of the writings of living poets, we shall be pardoned in this instance for deviating from our design, when we inform our readers that the following has been sent, as an unpublished poem of the late James Montgomery.

FATHER, thy will, not mine, be done,
So prayed on earth thy suffering Son ;
   So, in his name, I pray ;
The spirit fails, the flesh is weak,
Thy help in agony I seek ;
   O take this cup away !

If such be not thy sovereign will,
Thy better purpose then fulfil,
   My wishes I resign;
Into thine hands my soul commend,
On thee for life or death depend;
   Thy will be done, not mine!

———◆◇◆———

THE BEAUTIFUL.

BY EDWIN HENRY BURRINGTON,

A TRUE poet, as the following beautiful production sufficiently·
testifies.

WALK with the Beautiful and with the Grand,
   Let nothing on the earth thy feet deter;
Sorrow may lead thee weeping by the hand,
   But give not all thy bosom-thoughts to her:
                     Walk with the Beautiful.

I hear thee say, " The Beautiful! what is it?"
   O, thou art darkly ignorant! Be sure
'Tis no long weary road its form to visit,
   For thou canst make it smile beside thy door:
                     Then love the Beaut iful

Ay, love it; 'tis a sister that will bless,
   And teach thee patience when the heart is lonely;
The angels love it, for they wear its dress,
   And thou art made a little lower only:
                     Then love the Beautiful!

Sigh for it!—clasp it when 'tis in thy way,
   Be its idolator, as of a maiden!
Thy parents bent to it, and more than they;
   Be thou its worshipper. Another Eden
                     Comes with the Beautiful!

Some boast its presence in a Grecian face;
　　Some, on a favourite warbler of the skies:
But be not fool'd! where'er thine eye might trace,
　　Seeking the Beautiful, it will arise:
　　　　　　　　　Then seek it everywhere.

Thy bosom is its mint, the workmen are
　　Thy thoughts, and they must coin for thee: believing
The Beautiful exists in every star,
　　Thou makest it so; and art thyself deceiving,
　　　　　　　　　If otherwise thy faith.

Thou seest Beauty in the violet's cup;
　　I'll teach thee miracles!   Walk on this heath,
And say to the *neglected flower*, "Look up,
　　And be thou Beautiful!"   If thou hast faith,
　　　　　　　　　It will obey thy word.

One thing I warn thee: bow no knee to gold;
　　Less innocent it makes the guileless tongue,
It turns the feelings prematurely old;
　　And they who keep their best affections young
　　　　　　　　　Best love the Beautiful.

THE PICTURE.

THE following extracts are from a volume of far more than ordinary beauty, entitled "Alban," (London: Judd and Glass, New
Bridge Street,) by William Thurston. Had it reached us earlier
we should have made other quotations from this book, for its
pages are filled with beautiful poetry, and certainly deserves to be
better known. We see in this volume remarkable promise, and
believe the author to be a poet of whom Scotland (his native
country) will some day have reason to be proud.

HE saw the picture, started, glanced again—
Moved near to it, and lean'd his shaking form
Upon his staff, and with a troubled face

Gazed yet again ; and to his startled eyes—
All life left in him flew,—it seem'd the face,
The very face of her he loved in youth—
She lived his bride one year, and then she died
We take but one good treasure out of life,
And that is love : and she had gone to heaven
Laden with all the worship in his heart :
For forty years has grief lain on his soul,
And now in all her beauty she comes back,
The same as when both hearts were young and gay !
Again, amid her dancing curls he thrusts
His hand ; her merry laugh rings in his ear
As it was wont to echo through his halls ;
He sees the deep-brown eyes—sweet, loving eyes,
And ripe, warm lips ; ah ! yes, they surely smile
A loving recognition on him now !

DEATH.

AND Alban saw
Amid the frighten'd crowd a mother kneel,
Her arms around her children tightly flung,
Her face upturn'd to heaven—but that face
So pale, so death-like in its calm,—it seem'd
As if the soul had left and gone to God
To plead for her two babes.   One little one
Look'd o'er her shoulder on the crested waves,
And, pleased to see their foamy glitter, smiled !
One frenzied man, with careful hand, tied all
His gold about him, chuckling with a smile
To hear the yellow coins together ring !
One stood with terror dumb : one humbly pray'd :
One, weeping, prest a portrait to his lips :
A man, whose gold could buy an English town,
Knelt near a humble, toil-worn artisan,

Whose capital was nought but sinewy hands :
Each dreaded death, each cheek paled white with fear ;
And wildly throbb'd the princely man as he
Who had but life to lose ; for start which way
We will at birth, we all meet at the grave.

————◦◦◦————

THE VILLAGE CHURCH.

Its ancient low-built walls were thickly cloth'd
With clinging shrubs of gayest foliage ;
The Virginian creeper's graceful sprays
Hung o'er the Gothic windows' colour'd glass,
Darkening the dim figures of old saints.
Alban could see the one small bell swing to
And fro, calling the prayerful to God.
He went inside, and found it sweetly plain,
And rustic in its air.　Nothing was hid :
The grey-hair'd, toilworn sexton in the aisle
Stood tugging at the long bell-rope ;
A soft-eyed maiden on the organ play'd,
And a little village girl, most cleanly clad,
The organ bellows blew ; a rustic choir,
All simply dress'd, most heartily sang praise,
Not without music, though the tone was rough, —
All these were open to the view, and with
The frank-faced villagers fill'd all the place :
Except one lofty pew, into whose door
Alban had watch'd the beautiful young girl.

The pastor came ; a mild plain man, who gave
Discourse well suited to his humble flock.
When near its end he drew, the evening shades
Came softly down, and in all corners crept,
Till the fantastic faces carved around
The pillar tops, laugh'd more grotesquely still,

And seem'd to mock each other in the dusk;
The quaint Romaic letters on the wall
Were blurr'd and all unreadable;
The agëd peasants in the open seats
Were all commingled, and but dimly seen;
And as his tones grew low, the preacher's head
Threw a great shadow on the wall. At length,
The sermon ended, a parting hymn they sang,
In which a robin, who had stray'd inside,
And perch'd himself upon a lofty rail,
Joined with his clear, sweet notes, and strongly vied
In keeping up a stream of melody—
His little body quivering with joy—
Delighted to join man in praising God.

FAME.

"Do all
The teachers whom we reverence and obey—
Do all men look for praise as merit's crown?"

"Not all," he said, "for great souls are so wrapp'd
In the pure fire of their own noble thoughts,
That they forget their puny selves, and work
For naught but love of God and man; yet still
Some are but men of snow, and summer heat
Melts them away: they reach a giddy height
Of fame, and then withdraw their gaze from Heaven,
And cast their eyes around,—but he who stands
On pinnacles should never look below."

"Ah!" said she, drooping the lids of musing eyes,
"They may be right; and I, a simple girl,
May judge them wrongly; but methinks such spurs
Men need not seek. About an hour ago,
In yonder wood I heard the throstle sing;

And from the fulness of its joyful heart
It whistled strains so tuneful and so sweet,
With so glad music moving the rapt air,
And sending to the forest's deepest nooks
Quick-toned thrills and gushes of so mellow song,
That the tall trees with their still leaves did seem
To listen, and my heart could bless the bird
For giving earth so much more joy! It ceased;
And then, for very love of melody,
It started with its echoing song afresh:
Do men not work in their high art with some
Such pure delight?"

LOVE AND DEATH.

She died one pleasant eve: from a hedge near by
The scented May-blooms softly dropt, in sweet
And quiet sadness, on the reverent earth;
So sank she into death—she scarcely seem'd
To die—she look'd as much alive as when
She lived.   But love went with her like a cloud;
Love was her bright chariot to the sky;
Love open'd all the gates of pearl, and gave
Her added joy—e'en in the land of bliss!
And holy is such love—our Saviour smiled
With fondest eye upon his pupil John,
As smiles a mother on her new-born babe.

How rich is he who truly loves, and is
Beloved! he fears not all the ills of life,
Nor even death; for if but one true soul
Does cling in earnest love to him, then is
He never lost—then is he never dead!

LONDON: PRINTED BY W CLOWES AND SONS. STAMFORD STREET.

Uniform in size and price.

Fcap 8vo., cloth 3s. 6d., extra gilt 5s.   (*Post Free.*)

ROWLAND BROWN'S SONGS OF EARLY SPRING.

New and revised Edition.

ROWLAND BROWN'S LILY-LEAVES.

Second Edition.

ROWLAND BROWN'S BEAUTIES OF LYME REGIS.

Second Edition, Illustrated.

OPINIONS OF THE PRESS.

" ' Songs of Early Spring' are very beautiful."—*Illustrated London News.*

" Evidently the productions of a truly poetical mind."—*Tait's Magazine.*

" Poems far above mediocrity."—*Weekly Dispatch.*

" Delightful minor poems."—*News of the World.*

" ' Lily-leaves' exhibit the same freshness and purity of thought as ' Songs of Early Spring.' "—*Dorset County Chronicle.*

" Everything in this bouquet of intellectual sweets is fresh and spring-like." —*Weekly Times.*

" Warblings about bird, brook, and meadow, delightful love-poems and sonnets, making a most pleasant miscellany."—*Athenæum.*

" Rowland Brown's poems are far above average merit."—*Critic.*

"Rowland Brown's prose writings contain much poetry.   He eloquently describes the 'beauties' in which he evidently delights."—*Pulman's Weekly Times.*

LONDON : A. GOULD & Co., 13, BOUVERIE STREET, E.C.

"THE OLIVE-BRANCH."

Gilt edges, pp. 120, price 2s. 6d.

Poems, by William Stokes, Manchester.

London : JUDD & GLASS, Bridge Street. Manchester: G. HARRISON,
11, Cross Street, and the AUTHOR, 69, King Street.

OPINIONS OF THE PRESS.

" Here we have poesy of no mean order, dedicated to some of the noblest
themes that can thrill the soul of man. May these poems find their way to
many a home, and their spirit soon reign in every heart !"—*The Homilist.*

" We have gone through the work with unfeigned delight. There is a very
considerable amount of the true poetic fire burning in its pages. Peace is the
author's favourite topic. There are notes to some of the poems, containing
facts, at which the pulse almost stands still, so intensely demoniacal is the war
system of the world. With joyful haste we turn from them to the truly hal-
lowed aspirations for universal love, with which this book abounds."—*Primitive
Church Magazine.*

" The Author of this handsomely got-up little volume is well known as an
able writer in the cause of peace. The poems will be read and appreciated by
all who desire the promotion of the happiness of our race."—*The British Friend.*

" This little volume expresses some noble sentiments, and is characterised
throughout by earnest Christian sympathies: it contains also not a little excel-
lent poetry."—*The Freeman.*

" Some of the lyrics have touches of genuine pathos, and all are written in
smooth verse. Mr. Stokes has earned for himself a name by championing, at a
time when events scarcely indicate its feasibility, the notion of a permanent
congress of European nations as a substitute for war."—*General Baptist
Magazine.*

" We cordially commend his volume, for its soundness of principle, its earnestness of spirit, as well as its flow and felicity of versification "—*Herald of Peace.*

" Mr. Stokes is well known, in this county at least, as an earnest and eloquent
advocate of those great and glorious principles which have, not unsuccessfully,
inspired his muse. The poems will be read with pleasure and profit by all who
love freedom, and look for the day when wars shall cease. To all such this
little volume will be highly acceptable, and a valuable addition to their stock of
Christian poetry."—*Burnley Advertiser.*

BY THE SAME AUTHOR.
Just published, price Twopence,

A PERMANENT EUROPEAN CONGRESS:

ITS NATURE, AND THE MEANS OF ITS ACCOMPLISHMENT.

" We would earnestly recommend the general circulation of this well-written
pamphlet, not only throughout the United Kingdom, but in all the languages
of the civilized world."—*Primitive Church Magazine.*

P

A NEW CHURCH HYMN AND TUNE BOOK.

A MANUAL OF PSALMODY,

FOR THE

SUNDAY AND OTHER SERVICES

OF THE

Church of England.

BY THE

REV. B. F. CARLYLE,

VICAR OF CAM, GLOUCESTERSHIRE; AND

J. V. WATTS,

CHOIR MASTER OF ST. MICHAEL'S, BATH.

This Manual contains 250 Psalms and Hymns and 40 Doxologies, united to 125 appropriate Tunes; the Canticles, pointed for Chanting, and 75 Chants; 4 Sanctuses, 5 Responses, 4 Glorias, and a Choral Service for Daily Prayer and Litany, arranged from Tallis.

The work is so arranged, as generally to give the Two Tunes to each Hymn, and of Four Hymns, of the same general character to each Tune without the inconvenience of turning over.

Clergymen, desirous of improving the character of their Churches, are invited to test the special merits of this Work, specimens of which will be forwarded, on application, by the Publisher. This Manual is also, from its comprehensiveness, completeness, and moderate price, peculiarly adapted to Colonial and Missionary Churches.

PRICES OF THE VARIOUS EDITIONS.

		s.	d
1. Large paper Edition, handsomely bound in antique cloth, red edges		2	6
2. Small paper Edition, limp cloth, sprinkled edges . .		1	0
3. The Hymns and Doxologies only, limp cloth . . .		0	6 ʼ

All these Editions will be supplied in superior bindings at moderate prices.

Editions in larger type will be prepared with all practicable despatch.

The full allowance is made to Clergymen and others taking quantities; and the Publisher will be happy to give every facility for the introduction of the Book, by supplying any required number of copies on sale.

LONDON: J. HADDON, 3, BOUVERIE STREET, FLEET STREET,
AND BY ORDER OF ANY BOOKSELLER.

A LIST OF BOOKS

PUBLISHING BY

SAMPSON LOW, SON, AND CO.

47, LUDGATE HILL, LONDON.

[*November* 1, 1860.

NEW ILLUSTRATED BOOKS.

R. TENNYSON'S May Queen. Illustrated with Thirty-five designs by E. V. B. Small 4to. cloth, bevelled boards, 7s. 6d.; or in morocco antique, bound by Hayday, 1l. 1s.

A New Edition of Choice Editions of Choice Books. Illustrated by C. W. Cope, R.A., T. Creswick, R.A., Edward Duncan, Birket.Foster, J. C. Horsley, A.R.A., George Hicks, R. Redgrave, R.A., C. Stonehouse, F. Tayler, George Thomas, H. J. Townshend, E. H. Wehnert, Harrison Weir, &c. Crown 8vo. cloth, 5s. each; or, in morocco, gilt edges, 10s. 6d.

Bloomfield's Farmer's Boy.	Gray's Elegy in a Churchyard.
Campbell's Pleasures of Hope.	Keat's Eve of St. Agnes.
Coleridge's Ancient Mariner.	Milton's l'Allegro.
Goldsmith's Deserted Village.	Warton's Hamlet.
Goldsmith's Vicar of Wakefield.	Wordsworth's Pastoral Poems.

"Such works are a glorious beatification for a poet. Such works as these educate townsmen, who, surrounded by dead and artificial things, as country people are by life and nature, scarcely learn to look at nature till taught by these concentrated specimens of her beauty."—*Athenæum.*

The Poetry of Nature. Selected and Illustrated with Thirty-six Engravings by Harrison Weir. Small 4to. handsomely bound in cloth, gilt edges, 12s.; morocco, 1l. 1s.

Poems and Pictures : a Collection of Poems, Songs, and Ballads. Illustrated with Ninety Engravings on Wood, from Drawings by C. W. Cope, R.A., T. Creswick, R.A., W. Dyce, R.A., R. Redgrave, R.A., J. C. Horsley, R.A., F. Pickersgill, R.A., H. C. Selous, J. Tenniel, J. Franklin, H. J. Townsend, E. Duncan, F. W. Topham, E. Corbould, G. Dodson, J. W. Archer, C. H. Weigall; and Border Decorations on every page. A New Edition, with additional Ornaments. Crown 4to., handsomely bound in cloth, with ornaments designed by R. Dudley, with gilt edges, 1l. 1s.; morocco extra, 1l. 11s. 6d.

The Forest Hymn. By W. C. Bryant. Illustrated. Small 4to. cloth extra, 10s. 6d.

Our Little Ones in Heaven : Thoughts in Prose and Verse, selected from the Writings of favourite Authors; with an Introduction by the late Rev. Henry Robbins, M.A., beautifully printed by Clay, with Frontispiece after Sir Joshua Reynolds. Fcap. 8vo. cloth extra, 5s.

The Poetical Works of Thomas Gray. Illustrated with Eight Engravings by Birket Foster, and ornamented on nearly every page by Harry Rogers. Small square 8vo., handsomely bound in cloth, bevelled boards, 5s.; or in morocco, 10s. 6d.

Shakespeare's Merchant of Venice. Illustrated with Twenty large Engravings on Wood, from Drawings by George Thomas, Birket Foster, and Henry Brandling, and Decorated with numerous Emblematical Devices by Harry Rogers. Printed by R. Clay. Square 8vo., handsomely bound in Venetian ornamented cloth, gilt edges, 10s. 6d.; or in antique morocco, extra bound by Hayday, 1l. 1s.

The Novels of James Fennimore Cooper, Illustrated, now Publishing (Vols. I. to XVIII. ready). The Author's last and best Edition, printed on toned paper, with Illustrations on Steel from Designs by Felix O. Darley. The Volumes ready are—The Spy, Pioneers, Wyandotte, Bravo, Pilot, Red Rover, Last of the Mohicans, the Wept of Wish-ton-wish, The Headsman, The Prairie, Lionel Lincoln, The Sea Lions, Waterwitch, Homeward Bound, Monikins, Satan's Toe, Home as Found, and Pathfinder. Bound in cloth extra, each Volume containing a Novel complete, and sold separate, price 10s. 6d.

NEW BOOKS FOR YOUNG PEOPLE.

HE Children's Picture-Book of Birds and Beasts; with 120 Original Illustrations by William Harvey. 2 vols. Sup. roy. 16mo. cloth, gilt edges, each 5s.

The Children's Picture Book of the Sagacity of Animals. With numerous Illustrations by Harrison Weir. Super-royal 16mo. cloth. (*Shortly.*)

The Children's Picture Book of Fables. Written expressly for Children, and Illustrated with Fifty large Engravings, from Drawings by Harrison Weir. Square, cloth extra, 5s.; or coloured, 9s.

The Children's Picture Book of Country Scenes. By Harriet Myrtle. Illustrated with Fifty-five Engravings, from Drawings by Birket Foster, George Thomas, William Harvey, and Harrison Weir. Square 16mo., handsomely bound, gilt edges, price 5s.; or coloured, 9s.

The Home Treasury of Old Story Books and Ballads. Newly revised; with Sixty Engravings, from designs by C. W. Cope, R.A., T. Webster, R.A., J. C. Horsley, A.R.A., H. J. Townshend, &c. Square cloth extra, 5s.; or coloured, 9s.

The Seven Champions of Christendom. Re-written for Boys; by W. H. G. Kingston, Author of "Ernest Bracebridge." With Sixteen Illustrations by John Franklin. Square, cloth, 5s.

Favourite Pleasure Books for Young Children. Each printed on Thick Paper, and richly coloured in a style never before attempted at the price, from drawings by John Absolon, Edward Wehnert, and Harrison Weir. 6d. each, or, complete in one volume, with 100 superior Coloured Plates, cloth, gilt edges. 6s.

The Babes in the Wood. Illustrated by Lady Waterford, coloured in Fac-simile of the Original Drawings. Uniform with "Child's Play." Cloth, 5s.

Songs for the Little Ones at Home. Illustrated with Sixteen beautifully coloured Pictures by Birket Foster and John Absolon. Small 4to., cloth, gilt edges, uniform with "Child's Play," 5s.

Child's Play. Illustrated with Sixteen Coloured Drawings by E. V. B., printed in fac-simile by W. Dickes' process, and ornamented with Initial Letters. Imp. 16mo. cloth extra, 5s. The Original Edition of this work was published at One Guinea.

Fancy Tales, from the German. By J. S. Laurie, H. M. Inspector of Schools, and Otto Striedinger. Illustrated by H. Sandercock. Super-royal 16mo. cloth, 5s.

The Nursery Playmate. With 200 Illustrations, beautifully printed on thick paper. 4to. Illustrated boards, 5s.

The Babes in the Basket: a Tale of the West Indian Insurrection. With an Illustration. Fcap. cloth, 2s.

Difficulties Overcome; or, Scenes in the Life of Alexander Wilson, the Ornithologist. By Miss L. Brightwell, Author of "Heroes of the Laboratory," &c. With an Illustration. Fcap. cloth, 2s.

The Boy's Own Book of Boats. By W. H. G. Kingston, Author of "Ernest Bracebridge," &c. With numerous Illustrations by Edwin Weedon, engraved by W. J. Linton. Fcap. cloth, 5s.

Ernest Bracebridge: or, Schoolboy Days, by W. H. G. Kingston, Author of "Peter the Whaler," &c. Illustrated with Sixteen Engravings, descriptive of Schoolboys' Games and Pastimes, drawn by George H. Thomas, and printed in Tints by Edmund Evans. Fcap. 8vo. 5s.

The Voyage of the "Constance:" a Tale of the Arctic Seas. With an Appendix, comprising the Story of "The Fox." By Mary Gillies. Illustrated with Eight Engravings on Wood, from Drawings by Charles Keene. Fcap. 8vo. cloth, 5s.

The Swiss Family Robinson; or, the Adventures of a Father and Mother and Four Sons on a Desert Island. With Explanatory Notes and Illustrations. First and Second Series. New Edition, complete in one volume, 3s. 6d.

The Child's Book of Nature, by W. Hooker, M.D. With 180 Illustrations. Sq. 12mo. cloth, bevelled. 8s. 6d.

Actea; a First Lesson in Natural History. By Mrs. Agassiz. Edited by Professor Agassiz. Illustrated. Fcap. 8vo. 3s. 6d.

How to Make Miniature Pumps and a Fire-Engine: a Book for Boys. With Seven Illustrations. Fcap. 1s.

Geography for my Children. By Mrs. Harriet Beecher Stowe. Author of "Uncle Tom's Cabin," &c. Arranged and Edited by an English Lady, under the Direction of the Authoress. With upwards of Fifty Illustrations. Cloth extra, 4s. 6d.

The Boy Missionary; a Tale for Young People. By Mrs. J. M. Parker. Contents:—Chapter I. What can Davie do?—II. The Way opens. —III. The Work begins.—IV. Planting the Seed.—V. The First Frost. —VI. Poor Jack.—VII. Signs of the Harvest.—VIII. It looks like a Storm.—IX. It clears away.—X. Reaping Time. Fcap. 8vo. cloth, 1s. 6d.

FAMILY READING SERIES.

HE Household Library of Tale and Travel; a Series of Works specially adapted for Family Reading, District Libraries and Book Clubs, Presentation and Prize Books:—

1. Thankfulness; a Narrative. By Charles B. Tayler, M.A. 4th Edition. 3s. 6d.
2. Earnestness; a Sequel. By the Same. Third Edition. 3s. 6d.
3. Truth; or, Persis Clareton. By the Same. 2s. 6d.
4. Recollections of Alderbrook. By Emily Judson. 3s. 6d.
5. Tales of New England Life. By Mrs. Stowe. 2s. 6d.
6. Sunny Memories in Foreign Lands. By the Same. 2s. 6d.
7. Shadyside; a Tale. By Mrs. Hubbell. 3s. 6d.
8. Memorials of an Only Daughter. By the Same. 3s. 6d.
9. The Golden Sunset. By Miss Boulton. 2s. 6d.
10. Mabel Vaughan. By the Author of " The Lamplighter." 3s. 6d.
11. Types of Womanhood. By the author of " Ethel." 2s. 6d.
12. The Hills of the Shatemuc. By Miss Warner. 2s. 6d.
13. The Nun. By Mrs. Sherwood. 2s. 6d.
14. The Unprotected; a Narrative. By a London Dressmaker. 5s.
15. Dred; a Tale of the Great Dismal Swamp. By Mrs. Stowe. 2s. 6d.
16. Swiss Family Robinson, and Sequel. Complete edition, 3s. 6d. Illustrated.
17. Legends and Records. By Chas. B. Tayler, M.A. 3s. 6d.
18. Records of a Good Man's Life. By the Same. 3s. 6d.
19. Life Allegories and Similitudes. By Dr. Cheever. 2s. 6d.
20. The Fools' Pence, and other Narratives of Every-day Life. Illustrated, cloth, 3s. 6d.; or in stiff cover, 2s. 6d.
21. The Boy Missionary. By Mrs. J. M. Parker. 2s. 6d.; or in stiff covers, 1s. 6d.

*** The above are printed in good type and on the best paper, bound in cloth, gilt back; each work distinct and sold separately.

IN LITERATURE AND WORKS OF REFERENCE.

HE British Catalogue of Books Published during 1859 —21st Year. Compiled by SAMPSON LOW. In two parts. Part I. The full title-page of every work published in Great Britain during the year, with the size, price, publisher, and month of publication. Part II. An Index of Subjects, showing at one view all that has been published upon any given subject. 8vo. 6s. 6d.

Index to the Subjects of Books published in the United Kingdom during the last Twenty Years—1837-1857. One vol. royal 8vo. Morocco, 1l. 6s.

Although nominally the Index to the British Catalogue, it is equally so to all general Catalogues of Books during the same period, containing as many as 74,000 references, under subjects, so as to ensure immediate reference to the books on the subject required, each giving title, price, publisher, and date.

Two valuable Appendices are also given—A, containing full lists of all Libraries, Collections, Series, and Miscellanies—and B, a List of Literary Societies, Printing Societies, and their Issues.

An Index to Current Literature, comprising a Reference, under
Author and Subject, to every Book published in the English Language
during the quarter: each Reference giving Size, Price, Publisher, &c.;
also to Articles in Science, Literature, and Art, in Serial Publications,
including the "Times" Newspaper, the Weekly, Monthly, and Quarterly
Reviews, &c. &c. By SAMPSON LOW. Subscription, including postage,
4s. 4d. per annum.

    *** The first year's Subscription entitles Subscribers to the issue of 1
to 4 for the whole of 1859, in one alphabet, and in future the Publication
will be continued Quarterly.

The American Catalogue, or English Guide to American Literature; giving the full title of original Works published in the United
States of America since the year 1800, with especial reference to the
works of interest to Great Britain, with the size, price, place, date
of publication, and London prices. With comprehensive Index. 8vo.
2s. 6d. Also Supplement, 1837-60. 8vo. 6d.

The Publishers' Circular, and General Record of British and
Foreign Literature; giving a transcript of the title-page of every work
published in Great Britain, and every work of interest published abroad,
with lists of all the publishing houses.
    Published regularly on the 1st and 15th of every Month, and forwarded
post free to all parts of the world on payment of 8s. per annum.

    *** *Established by the Publishers of London in* 1837.

The Handy-book of Patent and Copyright Law, English and
Foreign, for the use of Inventors, Patentees, Authors, and Publishers.
Comprising the Law and Practice of Patents, the Law of Copyright of
Designs, the Law of Literary Copyright. By James Fraser, Esq. Post
8vo. cloth.

A Concise Summary of the Law of English and French Copyright
Law and International Law, by Peter Burke. 12mo. 5s.

An Enlarged Dictionary of the English Language. By Dr.
Worcester. Royal 4to., cloth. 1l. 11s. 6d.

    In announcing this work, upon which the author has been unceasingly
engaged since 1846, the publishers are fortified in their expectation of in-
troducing the most valuable and comprehensive Dictionary of the English
Language to the public that has yet appeared by the verdict of some of
the first philologists of the day. That it is a marvel of industry, superior
manufacture, and skill, they can testify by the mere comparison of the
book with any similar work.

    It contains 400 pages more than the Quarto Dictionary of Dr. Webster,
and 42,000 more words than Dr. Todd's Edition of Johnson.

    It comprises 1834 pages large quarto, in a good bold Type and upon ex-
cellent Paper, substantially bound in cloth, for One Guinea-and-a-half.

Lectures on the English Language. By the Hon. George P.
Marsh, late U. S. Ambassador at Constantinople. 8vo. Cloth, 16s.

EDUCATIONAL.

EOGRAPHY for my Children, by Mrs. H. B. Stowe.
Fifty Illustrations. Sq. 8vo. 4s. 6d.

A System of Physical Geography, by D. M. Warren.
With Coloured Maps. 4to. 7s. 6d.

Latin-English Lexicon, by Dr. Andrews. 7th Edition. 8vo. 18s.

A Manual of the Chaldee Language ; containing a Chaldee Grammar, chiefly from the German of Professor G. B. Winer. By Elias Riggs, D.D. Second Edition, revised. Post 8vo. cloth, 7s. 6d.

The Grammar of English Grammars ; Historical and Critical, by Goold Brown. Second Edition. 8vo. 25s.

First Book in Composition, by F. Brookfield. 18mo. 2s. 6d.

Art of Elocution, with a Modern Speaker, by George Vandenhoff. Second Edition. 12mo. 5s.

The Laws of Life, with especial reference to the Education of Girls. By Elizabeth Blackwell, M.D. New Edition, revised by the Author, 12mo. cloth, 3s. 6d.

Letters to the People, on Health and Happiness ; by Catherine E. Beecher. Illustrated. 12mo. 3s. 6d.

Physiology and Calisthenics ; by the same Author. Illustrations. 12mo. 3s. 6d.

Select British Eloquence, by Chauncy A. Goodrich. 8vo. cl. 18s.

HISTORY AND BIOGRAPHY.

LUTARCH'S Lives. An entirely new Library Edition, carefully revised and corrected, with some Original Translations by the Editor. Edited by A. H. Clough, Esq. sometime Fellow of Oriel College, Oxford, and late Professor of English Language and Literature at University College. 5 vols. 8vo. cloth. 2l. 10s.

The Life, Travels, and Books of Alex. Von Humboldt. With an Introduction by Bayard Taylor, Author of "Life and Landscapes in Egypt," &c. In one vol. post 8vo. cloth, 8s. 6d. with portrait on steel.

The Life of General Garibaldi, the Roman Soldier, Sailor, Patriot, and Hero ; with Sketches of his Companions in Arms. Translated from his private MSS. by his friend and admirer, T. Dwight. With a Portrait on Steel. Post 8vo. cloth, 8s. 6d.

The Life of General Havelock, K.C.B. By the Hon. J. T. Headley, late Secretary of the State of New York. In one vol. post 8vo. cloth, 8s. 6d.

Public Economy of the Athenians, by Augustus Boeckh, from the 2nd German Edition. 8vo. 21s.

The Works of Josephus, with a Life written by Himself. Translated from the original Greek, including Explanatory Notes and Observations. By William Whiston, A.M. With a Complete Index. 4 vols. 8vo. cloth, 24s.

The Monarchy of France, its Rise, Progress, and Fall, by William Tooke, F.R.S. 8vo. New Edition. 7s. 6d.

A Diary of the American Revolution, from Official and Authentic Sources. By Frank Moore. With several Engravings on Steel, Maps, Plans, &c. 2 vols. 8vo. 1l. 10s.

George Washington's Life, by Washington Irving. Library
Illustrated Edition. 5 vols. Imp. 8vo. 4*l.* 4*s.* Library Edit. Royal 8vo.
12*s.* each

Life of John Adams, 2nd President of the United States, by C.
F. Adams. 8vo. 14*s.* Life and Works complete, 10 vols. 14*s.* each.

TRAVEL AND ADVENTURE.

THE Cottages of the Alps; or, Life and Manners in
Switzerland. By a Lady. Illustrated with the Crests of the
Cantons. 2 vols. post 8vo. Cloth extra, 21*s.*
  "*A valuable sketch of the present state of Switzerland.*"—
Examiner.
" *A book that has been long wanted.*"—Daily News.

A Journey into the Back Country, including an Exploration of
the Valley of the Mississippi. By Frederick Law Olmstead, Author of
" Walks and Talks of a Farmer in England," &c. 8vo. cloth, 8*s.* 6*d.*

The Prairie and Overland Traveller; a Companion for Emigrants,
Traders, Travellers, Hunters, and Soldiers, traversing great Plains and
Prairies. By Capt. R. B. Marcey. Illustrated. Fcap. 8vo. cloth, 3*s.* 6*d.*
  " This is a real, carefully executed collection of information and experiences, the which every one who takes up will hardly lay down until he has
read from A to Z. . . . . It is not only valuable to the special traveller, but
fascinating to the general reader. . . . . The author is as full of matter as any
old sailor who has sailed four times round the world."—*Athenæum.*

Ten Years of Preacher Life; Chapters from an Autobiography.
By William Henry Milburn, Author of " Rifle, Axe, and Saddle-Bags."
With Introduction by the Rev. William Arthur, Author of " The Success-
ful Merchant," &c. Crown 8vo. cloth. 4*s.* 6*d.*
  " The book must be a favourite by force of its talents, its stories, and its amusing variety."—*London Review.* " He is a capital storyteller, and anybody who does not heartily en- joy his book must be as unamusable as Louis XIV., when Madame de Maintenon found him so heavy on hand."—*Spectator.*

Travels in Greece and Russia. With an Excursion to Crete. By
Bayard Taylor, Author of " Summer and Winter Pictures in Sweden,
Norway, and Lapland." Post 8vo. cloth, with two Illustrations. 7*s.* 6*d.*

Summer and Winter Pictures of Sweden, Lapland, and Norway,
by Bayard Taylor. Post 8vo. cloth, 8*s.* 6*d.*

Waikna; or, Adventures on the Mosquito Shore. By E. G.
Squier, Esq. Author of " Travels in Central America." 12mo. boards.
Illustrated cover. Third Edition, price 1*s.* 6*d.*
  "*A narrative of thrilling adventure and singular beauty.*"—Daily News.

Southern Lights and Shadows; a book for intending Emigrants
to Australia, by Frank Fowler, late of Her Majesty's Civil Service, New
South Wales. Cloth extra, 2*s.* 6*d.*; or cheap edition, 1*s.* 6*d.*

The Merchant Abroad, by George Francis Train. Post 8vo. 8*s.* 6*d.*

The New and the Old; or, California and India in Romantic Aspects. By J. W. Palmer, M.D. Author of " Up and Down the Irrawaddi;
or, the Golden Dagon." Post 8vo. cloth. 8*s.* 6*d.*

The States of Central America, by E. G. Squier. Cloth. 18*s.*

A Health Trip to the Tropics, by N. Parker Willis. Post 8vo. 10s. 6d.

Canada and its Resources. Two Prize Essays, by Hogan and Morris. 7s., or separately, 1s. 6d. each, and Map, 3s.

Central Africa; or, Life and Landscapes from Egypt to the Negro Kingdoms of the White Nile, by Bayard Taylor. 7s. 6d.

India, China, and Japan, by Bayard Taylor. 7s. 6d.

Palestine, Asia Minor, Sicily, and Spain. By Bayard Taylor. (2nd Edition.) 7s. 6d.

Boat-Life and Tent-Life in Egypt, Nubia, and the Holy Land, by W. C. Prime. 2 vols. Post 8vo. 17s.

Letters from Spain and Other Countries in 1857-8. By William Cullen Bryant. Post 8vo. cloth. 8s. 6d.

The Attaché in Madrid; or, Sketches of the Court of Isabella II. From the German. Post 8vo. 7s. 6d.

At Home and Abroad, by Madame Ossoli Fuller. 7s. 6d.

Sunny Memories of Foreign Lands; by Mrs. Harriet Beecher Stowe. With 60 Illustrations. 2s. 6d.

Impressions of England, by the Rev. A. Cleveland Coxe. 6s.

SCIENCE AND DISCOVERY.

PHYSICAL Geography of the Sea; or, the Economy of the Sea and its Adaptations, its Salts, its Waters, its Climates, its Inhabitants, and whatever there may be of general interest in its Commercial Uses or Industrial Pursuits. By M. F. Maury, LL.D., Lieutenant of the United States' Navy. Eighth and cheaper Edition, with important additions, with Illustrative Charts and Diagrams. Crown 8vo. cloth. 5s.

" We err greatly if Lieut. Maury's book will not hereafter be classed with the works of the great men who have taken the lead in extending and improving knowledge and art; his book displays in a remarkable degree, like the 'Advancement of Learning,' and the 'Natural History' of Buffon, profound research and magnificent imagination."—*Illustrated London News.*

The Physical Geography of the Sea and its Meteorology. By the same Author, based on his first Work. 8vo. [*In Preparation.*

The Kedge Anchor; or, Young Sailor's Assistant, by William Brady. Seventy Illustrations. 8vo. 16s.

Theory of the Winds, by Capt. Charles Wilkes. 8vo. cl. 8s. 6d.

Archaia; or, Studies of the Cosmogony and Natural History of the Hebrew Scriptures. By Professor Dawson, Principal of McGill College, Canada. Post 8vo. cloth, 7s. 6d.

" It is refreshing to meet with an author who has reflected deeply, and observed as well as read fully, before he has put forward his pages in print. He will be remembered, and perhaps read, when incompetent writers have been forgotten. We heartily commend this book to intelligent and thoughtful readers: it will not suit others. Its tone throughout is good, while as much is condensed in this one volume as will be required by the general student."—*Athenæum.*

The Recent Progress of Astronomy, by Elias Loomis, LL.D.
3rd Edition. Post 8vo. 7s. 6d.

An Introduction to Practical Astronomy, by the Same. 8vo.
cloth. 8s.

The Bible and Astronomy, by Dr. Kurtz, from the 3rd German
Edition. Post 8vo. 7s. 6d.

System of Mineralogy, by James D. Dana. New Edit. Revised.
With Numerous Engravings. 2 vols. 8vo. 24s.

Cyclopædia of Mathematical Science, by Davies and Peck. 8vo.
Sheep. 18s.

The Canadian Naturalist and Geologist. 8vo. Bimonthly. 3s.

A Dictionary of Photography. By Thomas Sutton, B.A., Editor
of "Photographic Notes." Illustrated with Woodcut Diagrams. 1 vol.
crown 8vo. red edges, 7s. 6d.

The Practice of Photography; a Manual for Students and Ama-
teurs, by Philip H. Delamotte, F.S.A. 3rd Edition. 4s. 6d.

TRADE, COMMERCE, AND AGRICULTURE.

HISTORY of Coal, Coke, Coal Fields, the Winning
and Working of Collieries, Varieties of Coal, Mine Surveying,
and Government Inspection. Iron, its ores and processes of
Manufacture throughout Great Britain, France, Belgium, &c.
Including Estimates of the Capital required to embark in the
Coal, Coke, or Iron Trades; the probable amount of profit to be realised;
value of Mineral Property, &c. &c. By W. Fordyce, Author of a History of the County Palatine of Durham. Imp. 4to. cloth. 2l. 10s.; or, in
half morocco, 2l. 12s. 6d.

History of the Rise and Progress of the Iron Trade of the United
States, from 1621 to 1857; with numerous Statistical Tables relating to
the Manufacture, Importation, Exportation, and Prices of Iron for more
than a Century. By B. F. French. 8vo. cloth. 10s.

Opportunities for Industry; or, One Thousand Chances for
Making Money. By Edwin T. Freedley, Esq. Author of "A Practical
Treatise on Business," &c. One vol. 8vo. cloth. 6s.

" This is a better book than its title indicates; its name reads like quackery, but it is really a volume full of curious and instructive matter, and abounding with valuable admonitions." Shipping and Mercantile Gazette.
" We quote a favourable passage that refers to a subject of some interest at the present moment—' The Trade with Japan.' "*—Athenæum.
" This is something like a book. Who would be poor when by purchasing it he may have at his disposal not less than one thousand and twelve chances of making a fortune?"—Atlas.

Hunt's Merchants' Magazine (Monthly). 2s. 6d.

Pleasant Talk about Fruits, Flowers, and Farming. By Henry
Ward Beecher, Author of "Life Thoughts." In ornamental cloth, price
2s. 6d.
Full of pleasant and valuable information not usually met with in books.

The Midland Florist and Suburban Horticulturist, a Hand-book
for the Amateur and Florist, conducted by Alfred G. Sutton. Published
monthly, price 3d.

The Book of Farm Implements, and their Construction; by John L. Thomas. With 200 Illustrations. 12mo. 6s. 6d.

The Practical Surveyor's Guide; by A. Duncan. Fcp. 8vo. 4s. 6d.

ARCHITECTURE AND DRAWING.

ESIGNS for Parish Churches; with 100 Illustrations. By J. Coleman Hart. 8vo. cloth. 21s.

Villas and Cottages; by Calvert Vaux, Architect. 300 Illustrations. 8vo. cloth. 12s.

The Amateur's Drawing Book, and Basis of Study for the Professional Artist. By J. G. Chapman, M.A. With numerous Illustrations. 4to. cloth, gilt top, One Guinea.

Compositions in Outline. By Felix O. C. Darley. From Judd's Margaret. Folio. Originally published at Three Guineas. 1l. 1s.

THEOLOGY.

HE Land and the Book, or Biblical Illustrations drawn from the Manners and Customs, the Scenes and the Scenery of the Holy Land, by W. M. Thomson, M.D., twenty-five years a Missionary in Syria and Palestine. With 3 Maps and several hundred Illustrations. 2 vols. Post 8vo. cloth. 1l. 1s.

A Topographical Picture of Ancient Jerusalem; beautifully coloured. Nine feet by six feet, on rollers, varnished. 3l. 3s.

A New Biblical Chart of the History of the Jews. Compiled by Jane Brough, Author of "How to Make the Sabbath a Delight," &c. Lithographed by J. Unwin. 10s. 6d. on sheet; or mounted and varnished, on roller, 15s. Size 3 ft. 2 in. by 3 ft. 4 in.

Thoughts on the Services; or, Meditations before Worship. Designed as an Introduction to the Liturgy, and an Aid to its Devout Use. By Rev. A. Cleveland Coxe, Rector of Christchurch, Baltimore, Author of "Impressions of England." Revised for the use of the Church of England, by the Rev. Leopold John Bernays, M.A. Printed by Whittingham. Fcp. 8vo. cloth, red edges. 3s. 6d.

"*A warm-hearted suggestive work.*" English Churchman.
" We have been struck with the great amount of really useful information conveyed, and the pious and devotional spirit which breathes through the whole, and we think the volume will be found a most useful one to introduce into our parishes."—Clerical Journal.
" Any one who is acquainted with Mr. Cleveland Coxe's works will anticipate the character of his 'Thoughts on the Services.' Though by no means deficient in ritualistic information, the

book aims rather at presenting the devotional aspect of the services of the Christian year. This object it fulfils by its simple and affectionate tone." Guardian.

" The name of this author has been so often before the English public, and generally in association with works of considerable merit, that a very brief mention on our part will suffice to make our readers anxious to obtain this, his last and very best book." Literary Churchman.

A Short Method of Prayer; an Analysis of a Work so entitled by Madame de la Mothe-Guyon; by Thomas C. Upham, Professor of Mental and Moral Philosophy in Bowdoin College, U.S. America. Printed by Whittingham. 12mo. cloth. 1s.

Prevailing Prayer. With Introduction by Norman Macleod, D.D., Author of " The Earnest Student," &c. Fcap. cloth. 1s. 6d.

The Higher Christian Life. By the Rev. W. E. Boardman. Fcap. cloth. 1s. 6d.

The New Life. By Horace Bushnell, D.D. Crown 8vo. cloth, 4s. 6d.; cheap edit. 2s.

" A volume of profound thought and splendid eloquence. It displays the author's great powers in their happiest and most useful exercise."—*Edinburgh Courant.*

Christian Believing and Living. By F. D. Huntington, D.D. Crown 8vo. cloth, 4s. 6d.

" For freshness of thought, power of illustration, and evangelical earnestness, these writers [Dr. Huntington and Dr. Bushnell] are not surpassed by the ablest theologians in the palmiest days of the Church."—*Caledonian Mercury.*

The Power of Prayer, Illustrated by the wonderful Displays of Divine Grace during the American Revival in 1857 and 1858, by Samuel J. Prime, Author of " Travels in Europe and the East." 12mo. cloth. 2s. Cheap edition, 1s.

The Bible in the Levant; or, the Life and Letters of the Rev. C. N. Righter, Missionary in Egypt, Greece, Turkey, and the Crimea. By the Rev. Samuel Irenæus Prime, D.D., Author of " The Power of Prayer." Fcap. 8vo. cloth. 2s. 6d.

" Mr. Righter was the agent of the American Bible Society in the Levant, and, while there, engaged in much missionary enterprise in Egypt, Greece, Turkey, and the Crimea. Death overtook him in the prosecution of his labours. His journey to Jordan and Jerusalem, as recorded in these pages, is well deserving of attention. He seems to have been well acquainted with the countries over which he travelled, and his letters bear traces of single-mindedness and devotion." *Literary Churchman.* " We have read this volume with much interest. In addition to its being a monument to the memory of a pious, devoted, and successful labourer in the diffusion of God's Holy Word—suddenly called from his work to his reward—it contains lively descriptions of the countries and peoples of Paris, Switzerland, Italy, Greece, the Crimea, Turkey, Palestine, &c. But they are evidently descriptions given by a Christian man, who, while he observed and noted down much that was interesting, never for a moment forgot or neglected the great and important objects of his mission." *Wesleyan Times.*

God in the Dwelling; or, the Religious Training of a Household. By the Rev. Dudley A. Tyng. Fcap. 8vo. limp cloth, 1s.

Life Thoughts. By the Rev. Henry Ward Beecher. Two Series, complete in one volume, well printed and well bound. 2s. 6d. Superior edition, illustrated with ornamented borders. Sm. 4to. cloth extra. 7s. 6d.

Summer in the Soul; or, Views and Experiences of Religious
Subjects. By the Rev. Henry Ward Beecher, Author of " Life Thoughts."
In fcp. 8vo. cloth extra. 2s. 6d.

Communings upon Daily Texts, tending to a Life of Practical
Holiness. " Commune with your own heart."—Psalm iv. 4. Post 8vo.
cloth. 5s.

Life Scenes from Mission Fields; edited by the Rev. Hubbard
Winslow. Fcp. 6s.

Motives for Missions; Addresses by the Bishops of Carlisle and
Ripon, and others. Fcp. 8vo. 3s.

The Bible in England; by the Rev. C. D. Bell, Incumbent of St.
John's, Hampstead. 6d.

The Miner's Sons; Martin Luther and Henry Martyn, by the
same Author. 12mo. 1s.

Faith in Earnest; by the same Author. Fcp. 8vo. cloth. 1s. 6d.

A Complete Analysis of the Holy Bible, based on the Works of
the learned Talbot; by the Rev. Nathaniel West, D.D. Royal 8vo. cl. 30s.

Twelve Aspects of Christ; or, Christ All in All, by the Rev.
George Fisk, Vicar of Malvern. Fcp. 8vo. 4s. 6d.

The Rich Kinsman; or, the History of Ruth the Moabitess, by
the Rev. Stephen Tyng, D.D. Post 8vo. 5s.

The Life of the Apostle Peter; by the Rev. Dr. Lee, Bishop of
Delaware. Fcp. 8vo. 5s.

History of the Old Hundredth Psalm; by H. W. Havergall. 8vo.
3s. 6d.

Presbyterian Looking for the Church. Fcp. 8vo. cloth. 6s. 6d.

Sermons for all Seasons; by the Rev. Charles B. Tayler, M.A.
Fcp. 8vo. cloth. 5s.

Sermons for Family Reading; by the Rev. William Short, Rector
of St. George-the-Martyr, Queen Square. 8vo. cloth. 10s. 6d.

Sermons for Boys; or, the Church in the Schoolroom, by the Rev.
L. J. Bernays. Fcp. 8vo. 5s.

Professor Upham's Life of Faith, and Interior Life. 2 vols. 5s. 6d.
each.

Professor Upham's Divine Union. 7s. 6d.

Life and Experience of Madame de la Mothe Guyon. By Professor Upham. Edited by an English Clergyman. Crown 8vo. cloth, with
Portrait. Third Edition, 7s. 6d.

Life of Madame Catherine Adorna; 12mo. cloth. 4s. 6d.

LAW AND JURISPRUDENCE.

SUMMARY of the Law of Copyright and International Treatises; by Peter Burke. 12mo. 5s.

Elements of International Law; by Henry Wheaton, LL.D. 6th edit. royal 8vo. 31s. 6d.

History of the Law of Nations; by the Same. Royal 8vo. cloth. 31s. 6d.

Commentaries on American Law; by Chancellor Kent. Ninth and entirely New Edition. 4 vols. 8vo. calf. 5l. 5s.; cloth, 4l. 10s.

Lectures on the Constitutional Jurisprudence of the United States, by W. A. Duer, LL.D. 12mo. 10s. 6d.

Principles of Political Economy; by Francis Bowen. 8vo. cl. 14s.

Treatise on the Law of Evidence; by Simon Greenleaf, LL.D. 3 vols. 8vo. calf. 4l. 4s.

A Treatise on the Measure of Damages; or, An Enquiry into the Principles which govern the Amount of Compensation in Courts of Justice. By Theodore Sedgwick. Third revised Edition, enlarged. Imperial 8vo. cloth. 31s. 6d.

Mr. Justice Story's and his Son W. W. Story's Works,

Commentaries on the Constitution of the United States. 2 vols. 36s.
Familiar Exposition of the Law of Agency. Calf. 30s.
Bailments. 30s.
Bills of Exchange. Calf. 30s.
Law of Contracts. 2 vols. cloth. 63s.
Conflict of Laws. 8vo. cloth. 32s.
Equity Pleadings. Calf. 32s.
Equity Precedents, Companion to " Pleadings;" by G. I. Curtis. 8vo. calf. 30s.
Commentaries on Equity Jurisprudence. 2 vols. cloth, 56s. Calf, 63s.
Law of Partnership. 30s.
Promissory Notes. Calf. 30s.
Pleadings in Civil Actions. Calf. 25s.

MEDICAL.

HUMAN Physiology, Statical and Dynamical; by Dr. Draper. 300 Illustrations. 8vo. 25s.

A Treatise on the Practice of Medicine; by Dr. George B. Wood. Fourth Edition. 2 vols. 36s.

A Treatise on Fractures, by J. F. Malgaigne, Chirurgien de l'Hôpital Saint Louis, Translated, with Notes and Additions, by John H. Packard, M.D. With 106 Illustrations. 8vo. sheep. 1l. 1s.

The History of Prostitution; its Extent, Causes, and Effects throughout the World: by William Sanger, M.D. 8vo. cloth. 16s.

A History of Medicine, from its Origin to the Nineteenth Century.
By Dr. P. V. Renouard. 8vo. 18s.

Letters to a Young Physician just entering upon Practice; by
James Jackson, M.D. Fcp. 8vo. 5s.

Lectures on the Diseases of Women and Children. By Dr. G. S.
Bedford. 4th Edition. 8vo. 18s.

Principles and Practice of Dental Surgery; by C. A. Harris. 6th
Edition. 8vo. 24s.

Chemical and Pharmaceutical Manipulations; by C. and C. Morfit.
Royal 8vo. Second Edition enlarged. 21s.

POETRY.

NGLISH and Scotch Ballads, &c. An extensive Collection. Designed as a Complement to the Works of the British Poets, and embracing nearly all the Ancient and Traditionary Ballads both of England and Scotland, in all the important varieties of form in which they are extant, with Notices of the kindred Ballads of other Nations. Edited by F. J. Child. A new Edition, revised by the Editor. 8 vols. fcap. cloth, 3s. 6d. each, uniform with Bohn's Libraries.

Saul: a Drama, in Three Parts. Second Edition, post 8vo.
cloth, 6s.

The Painted Window; a Poem, by M. E. Arnold. Second
Edition, 3s. 6d.

Sabbath Haltings in Life's Wilderness; or, Sacred Poems for
every Sunday in the Year. By H. Outis. Fcap. 8vo. cloth. 4s. 6d.

Adventures of a Summer Eve; by W. G. T. Barter. 12mo. 6s.

Lee Shore and other Poems; by James M. Share. 12mo. 2s. 6d.

Poets and Poetry of Europe; by Henry W. Longfellow. 8vo. 21s.

Poetry of the East; by W. R. Alger. 8vo. 6s.

Codrus; a Tragedy, by Richard Neal. Fcap. 8vo. cloth. 2s. 6d·

Shakespeare's Tragedy of Hamlet: 1603-1604. Being the first and
second Editions of Shakespeare's great drama, faithfully reprinted with old-faced type on fine-toned paper, by Josiah Allen, jun. of Birmingham, from the Duke of Devonshire's celebrated copies, and dedicated, by permission, to his Grace. 8vo. cloth, 10s. 6d.; morocco, 21s.

POPULAR BOOKS AT POPULAR PRICES.

LICE CAREY'S Pictures of Country Life. 1s. 6d.
Angel over the Right Shoulder. 1s.
Boy Missionary; by Mrs. J. M. Parker. 1s. 6d.

Domestic Servants, their Duties and Rights; by a Barrister. 1s.

Dred; by Mrs. H. B. Stowe. (160th thousand.) 1s. 6d.

Fools' Pence, and other Tales; by C. B. Tayler, M.A. 2s. 6d.

Life Thoughts. By the Rev. Henry Ward Beecher. 2s.

Lights and Shades of Australian Life. 1s. 6d.

Mabel Vaughan; by the Author of "The Lamplighter." 1s. 6d.

Nothing to Wear, and Two Millions, by William Allen Butler. 1s.

Power of Prayer; by Dr. Prime. 1s.

Records of Alderbrook; by Emily Judson. 1s.

Rifle, Axe, and Saddlebags. 1s. 6d.

Shadyside; by a Pastor's Wife. 1s.

Tales and Sketches (complete); by Mrs. Stowe. 1s.

Truth; by Charles B. Tayler, M.A. 1s. 6d.

Waikna; or, Adventures on the Mosquito Shore. 1s. 6d.

Wolfert's Roost, and other Tales; by Washington Irving. 1s.

FICTION.

THE Professor at the Breakfast Table. By Oliver Wendell Holmes, Author of the "Autocrat at the Breakfast Table." New Edition. Fcap. 3s. 6d.

Types of Womanhood; in Four Stories. Reprinted from "Fraser's Magazine," "Household Words," &c. Story 1. Our Wish. Story 2. Four Sisters. Story 3. Bertha's Love. Story 4. The Ordeal. By the Author of "Ethel," "Sister Anne," &c. Fcap. cloth, fancy boards. 2s.

The Angels' Song; a Christian Retrospect. By Charles B. Tayler. With Illustrations. 5s.

Blanche Neville; a Tale of Married Life. By Rev. C. D. Bell. 6s.

The 160th Thousand of Mrs. Beecher Stowe's "Dred." 2s. 6d. Cheap edition, 1s. 6d.

Right at Last, and other Tales. By Mrs. Gaskell, Author of "Mary Barton," in 1 vol. post 8vo. 10s. 6d.

The Woman in White. By Wilkie Collins, Author of "The Dead Secret," 3 vols. post 8vo. Second Edition. 31s. 6d.

Antonina; or, the Fall of Rome. By Wilkie Collins, Author of "The Woman in White," &c. New Edition, in one volume, post 8vo. steel frontispiece by H. K. Browne, 5s.

The Eye Witness of Many Wonderful Things. By C. Allston Collins, Esq. With an Engraving on Steel by H. K. Browne (Phiz). Post 8vo. cloth, 5s.

Fiction—continued.

The Cruise of the "Frolic;" or, the Yachting Adventures of Barnaby Brine, R.N. By W. H. G. Kingston, Author of "Peter the Whaler." In 2 vols. post 8vo. 21s.

The Minister's Wooing : a Tale of New England. By the Author of "Uncle Tom's Cabin." Two Editions :—1. In post 8vo. cloth, with Thirteen Illustrations by Hablot K. Browne, 7s. 6d.—2. Popular Edition, crown 8vo. cloth, with a Design by the same Artist. 2s. 6d.

When the Snow Falls. By W. Moy Thomas. A Book for Christmas and the Fireside. 2 vols. post 8vo. 1l. 1s.

"A story book that will not quickly fall out of request. There is a delicacy of conception in the tales often poetical, and the carefulness of their execution is a comfort to all educated readers."—*Examiner.*

Round The Sofa, by the Author of "Mary Barton," "Life of Charlotte Bronte." 2 vols. Post 8vo. Second Edition. 21s.

Mabel Vaughan; by Miss Cummins, Author of "The Lamplighter." Edited by Mrs. Gaskell. Cloth, 3s. 6d. Cheap edition, 1s. 6d.

"Had we our will, the women of England should each possess a copy of 'Mabel Vaughan.'"— *Wesleyan Times.*
"We wish it success for the sake of the pure intention with which it was written. Mabel is a charming character, and one which may be safely held up for admiration."—*Saturday Review.*
"'Mabel Vaughan' is a quiet and intensely good story—the book is carefully written."—*Athenæum.*

*** In ordering this book, specify Mrs. Gaskell's Edition, as the Author has no interest in any other.

El Fureidis : a Tale of Mount Lebanon and the Christian Settlements in Syria. By Maria S. Cummins, Author of "The Lamplighter." Fcap. 8vo. 2s. 6d.—Also, Library Edition, Second Thousand, 2 vols. crown 8vo. cloth gilt, 10s. 6d.

"One of the best novels of modern times: a novel as rich in pure sentiment as it is in Christian philosophy, and as glowing in its portraiture of Oriental life as in its description of scenery."—*City Press.*
"The author has made good use of her material, and has shown both skill and industry: she has evidently taken great pains with her work."—*Athenæum.*
"A thoroughly good book."—*Morning Star.*
"The best novels. of which 'El Fureidis' is one."—*Glasgow Herald.*
"Not only has Miss Cummins enhanced her reputation by her present production, but literature has gained a valuable acquisition in this spirited and heart-stirring romance of 'El Fureidis.'"—*Leader.*